DANGER FOR
THE BARON

DANGER FOR THE BARON

JOHN CREASEY
as
ANTHONY MORTON

WALKER AND COMPANY
New York

First published in the United States of America
in 1974 by the Walker Publishing Company, Inc.

Published simultaneously in Canada by Fitzhenry
& Whiteside, Limited, Toronto.

ISBN: 0-8027-5297-7

Library of Congress Catalog Card Number: 73-93927

Printed in the United States of America.

10 9 8 7 6 5 4 3 2 1

CONTENTS

CHAPTER I

BLANK CHEQUE

" Oh, yes," said Daniel Farley, " I am quite serious, Mr. Mannering. My client is anxious to get these jewels for his collection. He knows—and I know—of no one more likely than you to get them for him and to deal with scrupulous honesty. You see what it is to have such a reputation."

He smiled. He was small and silver-haired, had a pink face which seemed unlined until one looked closely into it, and merry blue eyes—the kind of face which might have belonged to a comedian on the halls rather than to a respected London solicitor. His office was lined with varnished shelves and on them were black deed boxes and documents tied with red and white tape, yet the sun which shone through the tall, narrow window behind his chair showed up no dust on shiny varnish or on the large desk. The polished mahogany reflected his pale hands, starched white cuffs and gold cuff-links, as he held his hands together before him.

" So I have a reputation," murmured John Mannering.

" And now you are trying to make one for modesty," said Farley. " My instructions were most precise. I was to find a man who was an expert on jewels, who could buy in the course of business, who could be trusted with a blank cheque." He smiled again. " It amounts to a blank cheque, Mr. Mannering. The important thing is to find these jewels, make sure they are those which my client wants and buy them whatever the price."

" Even double their value ? "

" Even treble their value," said Farley earnestly, " although of course if you can obtain them at a fair price, my client will be happier."

"And I'm not to know who your client is."

"Is that so unusual? I am acting for him. He knows that I hope you will undertake the commission. He has heard of Quinns, of course—is there anyone in the world interested in precious stones or *objets d'art* who hasn't? Yours is the most fascinating shop I've ever visited, Mr. Mannering—every time I come, I wish I were a wealthy man!" Farley withdrew his hands from the desk, opened a drawer and took out a blotting pad; on the pad was a cheque book and a small document. "For your trouble, you will receive five per cent of the price paid for the jewels and as the total will probably not be less than a hundred thousand pounds, I hope that will be an inducement even for the owner of Quinns."

"Quite an inducement," agreed Mannering.

Farley stretched out a hand towards a pen which stood in a silver inkstand.

"So you accept? I will make out a cheque for fifty thousand pounds which you can place to your credit immediately, and give you a blank cheque which you can fill in provided it is for a sum not in excess of another fifty thousand." Farley picked up the pen. "Here is a simple agreement for you to sign, as receipt, and—a formality only—as an undertaking to use your best endeavours."

"Don't make it out yet," protested Mannering mildly.

He didn't say why, and Farley didn't ask, just replaced the pen, and sat back. He gave the impression of being a man whom life could never disappoint.

Mannering gave a similar impression of serene self-assurance. He was a tall, lean man whom even the cynics agreed was handsome. A few flecks of grey showed in his dark, wavy hair, but only at the temples. His eyes were hazel, eyebrows and lashes dark, and as yet there was no grey in his close-clipped moustache. He was tanned by the Swiss sun, had been back in England for only two weeks after a business trip which had taken him into the mountains. The tan made his eyes seem brighter; they were bright with curiosity just now.

"I like to know whom I'm working for," he said.

" I'm afraid that would be impossible, in this case."

" I'd like to know why he is so anxious to get these jewels, even if he has to pay through the nose for them."

" Collectors of precious stones, as you know well, are apt to allow their enthusiasm to run away with them," Farley reminded him. " He is an extremely wealthy man and can afford to indulge his whims."

" He wouldn't be after stolen gems, would he ? " murmured Mannering.

Daniel Farley appeared to be more amused than shocked. He clasped his hands together again and leaned against the desk, studied Mannering closely and then spoke with great deliberation.

" The one disadvantage, if it is a disadvantage, in having you to buy these jewels is your secondary occupation, Mr. Mannering. The—ah—detective in you asks so many questions, sees grounds for suspicion where in fact there are none. I know that Scotland Yard often consults you about jewel-thefts, I know that you have occasionally taken it upon yourself to investigate theft and other crime independently of the Yard—and that you have quite a remarkable reputation in the sphere of detection, also. But I have no reason to believe that these jewels were stolen, no reason to believe that you will find any obstacle to buying, except the obstinacy of the owners of the jewels." He paused ; did his fingers clasp a little more tightly together ? " After all, if in the course of your endeavours you should find any reason to think that anything criminal is involved, you could withdraw. I am not asking you to guarantee success, only to try."

No lawyer in London had a better name.

" All right," said Mannering, " I'll see what I can do."

Farley did not try to hide his satisfaction, signed the cheques with a flourish, blotted them and handed them across the desk. Mannering read and signed the receipt. Then Farley opened the drawer again, took out a manilla folder, and became expansive ; if he hadn't known the lawyer, Mannering could have become suspicious.

" Excellent, Mr. Mannering, I know my client will be

delighted.   And we want to give you all the help we can. Here are photographs of the jewels, which are diamonds, emeralds and rubies, with details of the weight of each stone, dimensions and peculiarities.   I know enough about precious stones to realise these are exceptional.   Here, also, are three names and addresses—each of a person who is believed to own some of the gems.   If they haven't them now, they did have some time ago."

" How long ago ? "

" Within the past twelve months, I think.   I'm not sure."

" Have they been asked to sell ? "

" You'd hardly expect me to know," said Farley.   He handed the folder across, obviously expecting Mannering to open it.   Mannering put it down, folded the cheques and put them in his wallet, then pushed his chair back.

" Has your client tried to buy them ? "

" He has made tentative inquiries but is sure he cannot buy them himself—if that weren't so, he would hardly be prepared to pay a handsome commission."   Farley made it clear that he wouldn't go further into that.   It would be a waste of time trying to make him.

" Will you be here if I need to refer anything back ? " Mannering asked.

" During the week, from ten o'clock until a little after five, yes.   During the evenings or week-ends you will usually find me at my home—The Lawn, Lynton Avenue, Guildford ; it's in the folder."   Farley stood up and rounded the desk.   " Let me repeat, I'm delighted.   It is a matter of real importance for my client."   He put a hand on the handle of the door.   " Forgive me for adding one more thing, Mr. Mannering.   It goes without saying that you will be using the utmost discretion, it is a confidential matter."

" You mean, I won't farm the job out ? "

" Yes."

" Personal attention guaranteed," murmured Mannering, and Farley's smile matched his.

Mannering wasn't smiling as he walked along Chancery Lane towards Fleet Street or as he turned right past the

Gothic mass of the Law Courts or along the Strand. He was only vaguely aware of the throbbing traffic and the crowded pavements. It was half past twelve, the April day was sunny and warm, restaurants and cafés were crowded, a steady stream of office workers turned down the narrow streets towards the Thames and the Embankment Gardens. Mannering was taller than most and many women looked at him intently, but he would probably not have noticed even had one had the beauty of Cleopatra.

There was going to be a sting in the tail of this job ; at least, there might be.

He took a taxi from Aldwych to Hart Row, a narrow turning off Bond Street. One end of Hart Row had been demolished by bombs, but a few exclusive shops were left, and the smallest of these was Quinns. In the one narrow window, against a background of dark blue velvet was a single jewelled casket said to have belonged to the Shah Jehan before the death of Mumtaz his Queen and the building of the Taj Mahal. A young couple, arm in arm, were looking at it, less with longing than with wonder.

Mannering went into the long, narrow shop. Two special lights were on, two men studied some of the rare pieces, oblivious of Mannering. Sylvester, the assistant manager, was at the back of the shop, a grey-haired, willowy man with the courtliness of a bygone age, wearing a morning suit, a winged collar and grey cravat. Sylvester knew better than to harass clients as they browsed, and his voice was hushed.

" Mrs. Mannering telephoned, sir, to say that her evening engagement has been cancelled."

" Oh. Thanks."

" There have been no other messages."

" Good," said Mannering. " I think I'll have some lunch sent in, about one."

" Very good, sir."

Mannering went on to the small office on the right of the shop. Beyond was a square hall, from which led a flight of old oak stairs, with two turns in them ; upstairs were the storerooms and small picture gallery. The office had just

room for his desk, which was two hundred years old but
modern compared with the premises. Shelves, crammed
with books, lined the walls ; a small safe stood in one corner,
over the hatch which led to the strong-rooms below.
Opposite Mannering was a portrait of himself, painted by
his wife, who had had it hung just there, so that whenever
he glanced up he would see himself as she saw him. He
seldom looked at it without picturing Lorna, too.

In the painting she had caught the faint smile that was
almost habitual, the gleam in his eyes, the hint of dare-
devilry which often showed ; and to amuse him and enter-
tain herself, she had dressed him in the picturesque coat, the
high stock and the bright colours of the Regency period.

" Where you really belong," she had said when she had
let him see it for the first time.

He didn't glance at it, but sat down, opened the file and
studied the photographs. There were three sheets ; all of
them were old and yellow at the edges and had been frequently handled. Beneath each jewel or piece of jewellery
were the dimensions, description of the setting, weight—
everything Farley had told him would be there. The
jewels were more remarkable for their perfection than for
their size—and it was easy to imagine the fiery brilliance of
the real things.

In each of the three sets there was a pendant, earrings,
bracelet and two brooches, all star-shaped ; and each with
three jewels, also star-shaped, which would fasten on to a
tiny cap of velvet or silk. Any women wearing a set would
be adorned with rare beauty ; anything more, and she would
be too heavily jewelled ; anything less, and she would be
less than perfect.

Mannering, who knew jewels as some connoisseurs know
old masters, had neither seen nor heard of them.

He took several thick, leather-bound volumes from a shelf
and one loose-leaf binder. He ran through this first—a
complete record of jewels which had been reported stolen to
Scotland Yard, including many stolen from overseas ; there
were hundreds of sheets. He turned each one over, swiftly ;
only twice did he need to pause, to check them against

Farley's photographs—and then the similarity was super-
ficial.

He opened the other books, containing photographs and
data about known private collections ; museum and gallery
collections ; and sets which had been sold privately or at
auctions. He found nothing resembling the jewels he had
been commissioned to buy.

He studied the names and addresses from the folder,
memorising them. None was a known collector of precious
stones.

William Blane, Esq.
17, Maberley Square,
London, W.1.

Lady Jane Creswell,
The Manor House,
Nr. Guildford, Surrey.

Mr. Aristotle Wynne,
Polgissy,
Cornwall.

Sylvester came in with Mannering's lunch from a nearby
restaurant which boasted a chef who lived for gourmets.
The chef would have been disappointed in Mannering that
day, for he ate absently and did not smile even when he
glanced absently at the portrait. He was less uneasy than
puzzled.

He pencilled the names and addresses on a slip of paper,
and rang for Sylvester.

" Would you like a liqueur, sir ? "

" No, thanks. Ought I to see anyone who's due in this
afternoon ? "

" Not to my knowledge, Mr. Mannering."

" Good ! As soon as Larraby gets back from the Portman
Square sale, give him this list and ask him to find out if
any of the people on it are known anywhere in the trade.

I don't want him to go too deep—just treat it casually and keep away from the police."

" I'll tell him, sir."

" If I'm wanted urgently," Mannering said, " I'll be at the first address, 17, Maberley Square."

CHAPTER II

THE HOUSE IN MABERLEY SQUARE

ONLY the wealthy lived in Maberley Square. None of the narrow-fronted houses, some plain brick and some faced with plaster, had been taken over by professional men or business houses. Most had been built in early Georgian days, some had small iron railings and tiny balconies on the first floor, none was exactly like the next—the shapes of windows, doorways and fanlights were different. The square was not large, the patch of lawn on the middle was protected neither by fences nor by *Keep Off the Grass* notices. There was no through traffic, for one end was a cul-de-sac, a mews in which stables had been turned into lock-up garages.

A little after two-thirty Mannering drew up outside Number 17, in his black Rolls-Bentley. He switched off the engine and a hush seemed to fall upon the backwater. It was more than pleasant, it was delightful. At the windows of houses on either side of Number 17 were boxes filled with daffodils already in full bloom and tulips beginning to burst, showing promise of colour to come.

There was no window box outside William Blane's house. This had white walls and a black door with a gleaming brass knocker and letter box. The window frames were painted black ; so was the number on the white fanlight. The effect would have pleased the most jaundiced.

Mannering sat at the wheel of his car, lit a cigarette, and appeared to be interested in a small girl and two French

poodles on the lawn.   In fact, he watched the windows of
Number 17.   They were covered with net curtains, but he
would be able to see if anyone inside were close to them ; he
saw no one.   Why should anyone be watching ?   Why
make mystery where there was none ?   In his gentle way,
Farley had warned him not to do that.

Mannering got out, went to the door and rang the brass
bell, which gleamed as brightly as the letterbox and knocker.
He heard it ring ; then footsteps sounded—light and quick,
those of a woman.   He heard the catch of the door go back,
tossed his cigarette away, and prepared to smile.   A petite
maid, in black dress and white lace cap and apron, looked
up at him inquiringly.

" Good afternoon, sir."

" Good afternoon.   Is Mr. Blane in ? "

" I don't know, sir.   If you will come in, I'll find out."

The hall was larger than one might have expected from
outside, square, with oak-panelling, parquet floor and a
Dutch panel or a good imitation on each wall, two William
and Mary slung-seated chairs, an atmosphere that couldn't
fail to please.

The maid took Mannering's card, which said nothing
about Quinns.

" I won't keep you a minute, sir."   She went up the stairs
which led off to the right of the hall, opposite the front door,
her footsteps ringing clearly on bare polished boards.   Why
no carpet ?   Did that matter ?   Mannering studied the
Dutch panels ; they were originals, beautifully painted,
with all the richness of colouring of the Rubens period.
Judged by what little he had seen, William Blane was a
man both of wealth and taste.

The maid's footsteps had stopped ringing—she had gone
into a room where there was carpet.   Mannering heard no
voices, but it wasn't long before he heard her on the landing
again.   She came down quickly.

" Mr. Blane's secretary will be happy to see you, sir."

" Thanks," said Mannering.   The ' will be happy ' had
a nice ring about it.

" Upstairs, sir, please."

He led the way up.   On the landing, he let the maid pass him.   There were three doors in sight, a passage and, beyond it, a flight of stairs to the next and top floor.   The maid tapped at the nearer of two doors on the right, opened it and announced him.   Mannering went in, not knowing what to expect—but knowing at once that he hadn't expected William Blane's secretary to look as she did.

She was young, she wore a canary yellow jumper which moulded her figure so perfectly that it might almost have been painted on, and a long black pleated skirt.   The high-necked jumper had short sleeves, finishing just above the elbows, and had nothing to relieve the plain colour.   Her glossy hair was as black as her skirt, braided and coiled to a knot at the back of her neck.   Her complexion was so flawless that it didn't seem real, and she wore no make-up ; her lips were faintly pink, their natural colour, but there was no colour at all in her cheeks.   She stood against a window, in front of a small desk with a portable typewriter on it, and in spite of the jumper she looked old-fashioned.

" Good afternoon, Mr. Mannering, please sit down." She had pushed up a chair for him, so that he sat at one end of the desk, and she took her own chair, pushed the type-writer away, and offered him cigarettes from an ebony box. " How can I help you ? "

Her voice was deep, slightly husky ; warm.

" I hope Mr. Blane is free to see me."

" Mr. Blane very seldom sees anyone without an appoint-ment, Mr. Mannering, but if you will tell me what it is about, I will ask him."

" He may be able to help me find some jewels that I want to buy."

The girl looked mildly surprised.

" Jewels ?   Could you be a little more precise ? "

She couldn't be.   Mannering found himself wanting to know more about her, whether this was her natural manner or one that had become natural ; or whether it was all pose.

" I can show Mr. Blane photographs of them."

" Perhaps if I were to take them into him, that would be quicker," said the girl.

" I'd rather do that myself," Mannering said, and hoped
that she wasn't as stubborn as she seemed. " If it isn't
convenient now, I'll make an appointment."

She hesitated, then stood up.

" Very well, I'll try." She turned away, going through a
doorway behind her chair, without tapping ; but she closed
the door on her flaring skirt. Mannering wasn't likely to
meet many girls like her in the course of a lifetime, but that
didn't make anything she said or did peculiar—everything
was normal, just a dutiful secretary protecting her boss
from nuisance callers.

Mannering had time to study the small room. The desk,
bookshelves on one side of it, and two filing cabinets, all
made of dark oak, made it partly an office. The corner
behind the door through which Mannering had entered was
quite different ; a small low table, two easy chairs covered
with flowered chintz, and a bowl of daffodils made it the
corner of a sitting-room. A copy of the *Saturday Evening
Post* lay on the table. Rust-coloured carpet covered the
floor from wall to wall.

Mannering also had time to finish his cigarette, and she
didn't come back. He heard no voices—sound had been
cut off when the door had been closed. In these old houses
doors were often thick but they seldom fitted so snugly.
Draught excluder on the other side probably explained that.

The door opened.

" Mr. Blane will see you," the girl said. She looked
surprised, spoke as if this were a rare privilege, and she didn't
smile ; she hadn't smiled, even faintly, from the moment
Mannering had set eyes on her. She stood by the door,
holding it open, and he said ' thanks ' in a muted voice
because everything seemed muted here, and went into the
next room.

William Blane sat in a large armchair in front of a blazing
log fire, the light from which flickered on the glass of bookcases which seemed to take up every inch of wall-space.
Unlined curtains were drawn at the long window, making
the firelight seem brighter. The man made no effort to
get up ; his right leg was stretched out stiffly, and a walking

stick lay against the chair, as if he couldn't move far without
it. That was not necessarily because of his stiff leg. He
was fat and short—he didn't need to stand up to show that—
with a tremendous paunch, big, flabby chin, eyes buried
so deep in flesh that they looked porcine. He wore a light
brown suit and the coat was unbuttoned ; the end of his
tie fell on to his paunch.

"Chair, Judy," he said in a tired voice. The girl was
already pushing up an armchair. "Sit down, Mr. Mannering. Can't get up easily myself." He paused, as if
breathless, between each short sentence. "All right, Judy.
I'll ring if I want you."

She went out and closed the door and the firelight flickered
on the roll of fat which buried Blane's chin, on the solitaire
ring on the little finger of his left hand, on his flabby face.
Yet he wasn't grotesque or repulsive ; and he wasn't old—
probably in the middle forties.

"Thanks," said Mannering, sitting down. "It is good
of you to see me. I don't expect to keep you long. I
am——"

"I know who you are," Blane said. "Mannering of
Quinns. Seen your pictures—had my agents buy some
oddments from you." He paused, giving the impression
that he was fighting for breath. "Never get about much
myself. Haven't for years. Heart. What's this about
jewels ? "

"I'm looking for some particular gems." Mannering
took the folder from his arm. "These——"

"What made you think—I could help ? "

"It's my job to find out who might," said Mannering
reasonably.

The answer probably didn't satisfy Blane, but he made no
comment. The light, although not good, was good enough.
Mannering handed over the first sheet of photographs.
He had no name for the jewels, no easy way of describing
them ; he might learn more here.

"These are some of them."

Blane took the sheet, turned it so that the light from the
fire fell on it, and studied the photographs. He showed

no expression, gave no hint that he recognised them.   He
looked as a figure of Buddha shown in contemplative mood
might look.   The dancing flames flickered over the glossy
surface of the photographs and darts of light shimmered
from his diamond.

Blane put the photographs down, resting it against his
stomach, looked levelly at Mannering, and asked bluntly :
"Who are you acting for ? "
"That's confidential."
"All right," said Blane, " all right."   He handed the
photographs back.   " I've the rubies.   No great objection
to selling—at a price.   But I'd want to be sure who was
buying them.   Sorry you've wasted your time."

He made that sound final, but didn't stretch out his hand
to touch the bell-push in the wall by the fireplace, and he
didn't look away from Mannering.   His short, breathless
sentences acted on Mannering much as Farley's manner
had done ; they offered a challenge.

"What price ? " asked Mannering.
"Does it matter, just now ?   Have your principal—
allow you to name him.   Needn't go any further until then.
Once I know that—I'll know whether I'll sell."

"Being sure you would sell might influence him."

"Perhaps it would," said Blane, " but I don't care a damn
if I sell or not.   Indifferent.   Jewels never appealed to me,
much.   No one to hang them on, anyway."   His lips
puckered into a smile.   " Except Judy—they wouldn't look
right on Judy."   He eased himself forward.   " Emeralds
would, mind.   Looking for the Korra emeralds, as well ?
And the diamonds ? "

"Are there diamonds and emeralds, too ? "   Mannering
hoped he sounded astonished.

Blane puckered his lips again, surprisingly gave a laugh,
not deep but well controlled, as if he were afraid to laugh
heartily.   It was almost *tee-hee-hee*.

"You know," he said.   " Go back to Jacob, tell him no.
Not while I live.   Just tell him that.   Stop wasting your
own time, Mannering."

"Jacob ? "

" You know who I mean."

" Wrong," said Mannering. I'm not dealing with a principal, only with lawyers."

" That right ? " asked Blane, as if surprised. " Bad habit, not knowing who you work for. Surprised at you." He was in a good humour, a much better humour than he had been when Mannering had arrived ; it was as if he were delighted that someone wanted to buy the rubies, and that he could say no. " Ask if the principal is Jacob Korra. K-O-R-R-A. If it isn't, come and tell me. I'd sell, but not to Jacob. Going to see anyone else ? "

" Who else might have the other sets ? " asked Mannering.

" Old Wynne, maybe," Blane said. His pauses were disconcerting, and he looked almost asleep. He was very wide awake. " Lady Jane ? " He grinned. " You know who's got 'em. Korra told you. From Korra, aren't you ? "

" No."

Blane didn't call him a liar, just looked what he thought.

" Prove it, and maybe I'll sell. Thanks for coming." He put out his left hand, the diamond sparkled and his forefinger touched the bell.

It was a form of dismissal that it would be difficult to ignore ; there wasn't any point in trying to argue with him yet. There would probably never be a time when argument would do any good. Some kind of a picture was beginning to form in Mannering's mind, and more lines were etched in when he stood up, as the door opened, and Blane laughed —*tee-hee-hee* again.

" Don't waste time with Jane, either ! Or money going down to Cornwall after Aristotle. Might as well try to make a deal with the original Arry. *Tee-hee-hee.*"

The light helped Mannering to hide his expression. He paused, with the girl by his side, to say that he didn't know what Blane meant. Blane just waved him away ; he was grinning, and didn't respond to Mannering's good-bye.

The girl, anxious to get Mannering out of the room, stood very close behind him. She closed the door as quickly as she could, and the smaller room seemed very bright.

" Tell Mr. Blane I'll gladly see him again if he should change his mind, will you ? " Mannering asked.

The girl named Judy looked at him intently ; and the green of her eyes was the green of emeralds, Blane had been right about the jewels best for her.

" He never changes his mind," she said, and seemed to have caught Blane's habit of speaking breathlessly. " Mr. Mannering, I——"

" Yes ? "

" I would like to see you, talk to you. Not here. May I telephone you ? "

She spoke as if it mattered, and were pleading with him— as if it were necessary for her to plead.

It was not a moment for questions, she was agitated and anxious—guessing why didn't help.

"What time?" Mannering asked. " I'll make sure I'm in."

" A little after six."

" I'll be at my Chelsea number," he promised. " If it's to talk, why not come straight there ? "

" I may not be free. I'll telephone." She still spoke softly, as if afraid of being overheard. " Thank you. I'll see you downstairs."

A bell rang on a long, subdued note. The girl glanced towards the door.

" Forgive me, Mr. Blane is ringing. The maid will see you out." She didn't smile, but Mannering got an impression that she was grateful, that she had expected him to say no. She opened the door; before Mannering went out, the bell rang again.

CHAPTER III

MANNERING WAITS

" DARLING," said Lorna Mannering.

Mannering, sitting in an easy chair, two evening newspapers on the floor by his side, had been staring into the fire.

" Mm ? "

" I could do with a drink."

" Eh ? Oh, of course." He stood up. " Sorry. Day-dreaming."

" Girl-dreaming."

" It's nearly seven," Mannering said, " I didn't think she would be late. She seemed too worried." He went to a Jacobean corner cupboard, almost black with age, which served the Mannerings as a cocktail cabinet in the Chelsea flat, above which was Lorna's studio. The room was large, every piece of furniture was an antique, every-thing else had Lorna's touch. She sat opposite his chair and watched him as he mixed the drinks—gin and Italian for her, whisky and soda for himself. He did this absently, and twice glanced at the telephone. He took the drinks to the fireside ; coke glowed red and spread a comfortable warmth. " Damned queer business. I don't like it."

" You're revelling in it."

He smiled down at her, raised his glass, and seemed to forget the girl named Judy and the silent telephone.

" Long life to the palette ! How's work gone today ? "

" Sweet of you to ask at last. Dismally."

" Too bad. Why ? "

" The same old trouble," Lorna said. " Satiation with painted, preserved or bucolic faces. I need a new model—or else you'll have to sit for me again, or lend me Josh. I think I'm in a mood when I could really paint Josh Larraby."

Mannering looked severe.

" It's past time you did a self-portrait. Now *there's* a model for you. Keep still, I'll describe it. A woman in the prime——"

" Darling, you make me sound like a joint of meat."

" . . . of life, the middle thirties, of rare beauty, superb grey eyes, raven black hair."

" It used to be, now the grey——"

" With a few strands of grey to add a touch of distinction, fine, broad forehead without a single line in spite of the ordeal of having a schizophrenic husband, complexion

superb if just a little darker than the true English rose,
lips——"
"I see them in the mirror every time I put on lipstick.
Are you sure this girl had on no make-up?"
"Positive. A little powder, not too much. No colour
at all. There's another model for you!" He sparked, as
if with enthusiasm. "Madonna and Mona Lisa, the two
in one."
"She certainly made a hit."
Mannering grinned, and glanced at his watch.
"It's certainly a quarter to seven and I like it even less
I wanted you to give her the once-over for me."
"You don't have to ask her to dinner. She can come
afterwards."
Mannering sat down, slowly, holding his glass carefully.
"I've an odd feeling that she won't telephone, and not
because she doesn't want to," he said. "Call me a fool."
"Fool," said Lorna.
She spoke quietly and stopped smiling, just watched him.
She guessed at the kind of thoughts that were passing
through his mind; she didn't like them but could do
nothing about them. They were quiet for five minutes, and
the telephone bell stayed silent. They heard the maid
moving about in the small dining-room, next to this;
dinner would be ready at seven precisely, for the maid
slept out.
"So you've that edge of a volcano feeling again," Lorna
said at last.
"More or less."
"I don't suppose I'll ever get really used to it," said
Lorna. "Sometimes I even wonder whether I'd be happy
if you lost the—" she hesitated and added deliberately—"the
gift. Was it always like this, darling? When the Baron
was at his wildest? Did you get the feeling that you'd
run into trouble when breaking into a particular house?"
Mannering chuckled.
"We'll get sentimental about the Baron if we go on like
this! No, I don't think so—if there's anything in this
sixth sense nonsense, it began after I'd put a life of crime

behind me and became a strict upholder of the law." The smile which Lorna had put into the portrait at his office glowed in his eyes, little more than a gleam, hinting at recklessness, daring, zest for life which couldn't be satisfied by the daily round.

He glanced at the telephone again. He didn't like the situation and couldn't really say why. Few were cursed or blessed with his kind of sensitiveness. In spite of his disclaimer, Lorna knew he had always been like it. In the days before they had met, a woman had turned him bitter and in a blind orgy of hate for mankind he had turned to crime. The quality that had set police and Press and public screaming after him was still within him. He had been dubbed the Baron after he had begun to enjoy the sense of being hunted, of matching wits with the police— and risking his freedom.

The man himself hadn't changed; only his motives.

Lorna had known him during the metamorphasis, when he had stopped robbing for its own sake, started to rob the rich and especially the unworthy, found himself righting wrongs for the excitement it gave him; then righting wrongs for its own sake. They were the excuse rather than the reason for action. Soon after he had met Lorna they had known their future would be together. The Baron had faded into the past, to emerge occasionally, as a substantial ghost; then fade again.

As the Baron, the police had hunted him; as John Mannering they had consulted him because of his knowledge of precious stones. Superintendent Bristow of Scotland Yard, who discovered that Mannering and the Baron were one and the same, fought personal liking while trying in vain to prove that he was right. It seemed so long ago but was vivid in Lorna's mind—she wondered how fresh it was in Mannering's, whether he ever regretted the changes.

At her suggestion he had bought Quinns. She had hoped without being optimistic that the business would bring an end to risks and danger. Instead, they had increased. As the owner of Quinns Mannering often worked with the police, as often independently of them, satisfying the odd, quixotic streak in his nature to help the lowly or those in trouble, always ready to damn the consequences.

Now and again, he was uneasy—often for no better reason than the silent telephone and the fact that Blane's young secretary hadn't found an opportunity to call.

The maid tapped and opened the door.

" Dinner is served, ma'am."

" Thank you, Ethel," Lorna said, and stood up. Mannering sat back in his chair. Lorna put her hands on the arms, leaned down, and pressed her lips against his, with a fierce, sudden passion. Then she straightened up and swung round.

" Dinner, darling." Her voice was choky.

" Yes, ma'am," said Mannering.

* * *

The girl named Judy hadn't telephoned.

It was after eleven o'clock. Lorna, who liked to get up early, had been in bed for half an hour. Mannering sat in his study with a book on his knees ; he'd read little since Lorna had gone. The uselessness of thinking over everything he had heard from Farley, Blane and the girl didn't matter—he couldn't keep his mind off it. There was no certainty that the girl had wanted to see him about the Korra jewels ; that was the trouble, there was no certainty about anything.

Josh Larraby, now his manager and right-hand man at Quinns, had been able to find out nothing about Blane or Lady Jane Cresswell ; Aristotle Wynne was a dealer in jewels in a modest way. There hadn't been much time, but if any of them had been well known, Josh would have found out by six o'clock, when he had telephoned from the shop. Mannering himself had made a few inquiries about the jewels ; no one he had spoken to had ever heard of them or heard of a man named Korra. He hadn't yet tried the police ; he would, soon, to satisfy himself that there was nothing known, criminally, about the mysterious Korra or the other three people. His disquiet was far greater than the circumstances seemed to warrant, which was no reason for rejecting it.

He put his book down and stood up. He might as well go to bed ; he would probably drop off to sleep. He had a sense of expectancy which he tried to ignore, poured himself a nightcap, lit a final cigarette, and was half-way through when the telephone bell rang.

He reached the instrument before it stopped ringing, glancing at his watch ; it was twenty minutes to twelve. He lifted the receiver, and the sense of expectancy was stronger than ever.

" John Mannering."

" Mr. Mannering," a girl said, and although her voice was pitched on a low key, as if she were anxious not to be overheard, its warmth came through ; this was Judy. " I'm sorry I'm so late, but *could* you come and see me ? It's Judy Darrow speaking, Mr. Blane's secretary."

She had pleaded before ; she was pleading now, but that was no reason for saying ' yes ' as if he were waiting to jump to her call.

" Tonight, Miss Darrow ? "

" I know it's unreasonable, but I haven't had a chance before. Mr. Blane—Mr. Blane has only just gone to bed, I couldn't get away. I doubt if I'll have a chance tomorrow, and I desperately want to see you."

" What about ? " asked Mannering, as if he didn't greatly care and wasn't likely to go.

" Those rubies—you were talking to Mr. Blane about them. That and other things. I can't go into detail here but if you could come——" she broke off.

" How did you know we were talking about rubies ? "

" There is a dictaphone in Mr. Blane's room, he likes a record of all conversations," said the girl, as if that were a trifle. " I do understand it's late, I wouldn't trouble you if I weren't so worried."

Mannering could ask her what she was worried about ; and probably she would try to explain even on the telephone. She couldn't guess that he would have gone, even if she had called up very much later. His voice still lacked enthusiasm.

"Well—I hope it won't take too long," he said. "Do you want me to come to Maberley Square?"

"Please. Don't ring the bell, I—perhaps I'd better leave the door open. I'll be watching from upstairs, and come down when I see you outside. I don't want any of the servants to know that—that I've a late visitor." She paused, sounded as if she knew that it wasn't very convincing, and went on: "I can't come out myself, Mr. Blane might ring for me at any moment."

"All right," said Mannering. "I'll be there in about twenty minutes."

"Thank you *very* much." The girl's relief was so great that it seemed unreal; like her appearance and like her manner.

Mannering rang off, but didn't move away from the telephone. Nine times out of ten a summons like that would have left him cold; or warned him of some trap. Why think of a trap, in this case? What could be wrong? An unknown client who wanted rare jewels which were little known, a fat man with a bad heart who had some of them but wouldn't sell to a certain Jacob Korra and obviously knew all about them; a young girl secretary with a load on her mind and who might be able to tell him more about the jewels—who was obviously under Blane's thumb, too, and desperately anxious that Blane shouldn't know that she wanted to talk to Mannering.

It was odd, but that didn't make it dangerous; did it?

He went into his bedroom. Lorna wasn't asleep. She guessed who had called, wasn't surprised that he was going out. He kissed her forehead lightly before going back into the study, opened a safe which was electrically operated and concealed in a carved Elizabethan oak settle, took out a small automatic, loaded it, slipped it into his pocket, then went out of the house and walked briskly to his garage, not far away. The gun was heavy against his side; now that he had it with him, he found it easy to laugh at himself.

CHAPTER IV

THE OPEN DOOR

THREE lighted windows showed in Maberley Square ; one of them was at Number 17. Mannering drew up at the far end of the square, turned the Rolls-Bentley to save trouble when he came away, and walked fifty yards along the narrow pavement towards the house. It was midnight ; the square was silent, no sound strayed to it even from Oxford Street and Park Lane, both quite near.

The night was dark.

His footsteps sounded loudly, seemed to echo. He looked up at the first floor window of the house and at the light, expecting to see the outline of the girl's head and shoulders against it. He saw nothing but the light and the pale-coloured net curtains. Now that he was nearer, he noticed a light in the hall, also—coming through the glass of the fanlight.

He turned the handle of the door and pushed, and it opened—just as the girl had arranged.

If he took Farley's advice, and followed his own reasoning, there was no reason to feel on edge, to be wary. Wariness was simply habit—a good habit. He stepped inside the hall, expecting the girl to come hurrying down ; nothing stirred. Shaded lights over the Dutch panels were on, not the main hall light. He stood quite still after closing the door without latching it, and listened ; no, nothing moved. He put his right hand to his pocket and the gun felt cold. He took his hand away as he stepped towards the stairs and looked up. There was no sign of Judy Darrow. Probably she had waited for a car, expecting him to drive straight up to the house. But had she been watching, she would have seen him— and heard his footsteps.

Halfway up the stairs, Mannering thought he heard

a sound, stopped abruptly, and dropped his hand to his pocket again. Imagination ? He heard nothing else, and started up again, but this time let his hand stay on the gun.

The landing was in darkness, only the faintest glimmer of light reached it from the hall. None of the doors leading off the landing was open. He looked at the door of the girl's office and living-room, and no light framed the door itself ; there should be a little if a light were on. He went to the door, opened it, and was met by darkness and silence.

The room with the light was across the landing.

He left this door open, and stepped across to the other, hesitating before he opened it. The light was bright. No sound came. He pushed the door back, and said quietly :

" Miss Darrow."

There was no answer.

He stepped into the room. It was spacious, beautifully appointed in grey and blue *decor*, but he spent little time studying that. The room was empty. The only sign that it had been occupied that evening was the dying fire, and the piano, open, with a sheet of music slipping off the stand—a little-known piece by Rachmaninoff. There was a faint smell of tobacco smoke. The big curtains were not drawn. A chair stood turned towards the window, in the position the girl would probably have been sitting, had she been waiting for him.

He went out.

He had been here five minutes, and whatever the girl had gone to do, she should be back by now. If he'd judged her manner correctly, she ought to have been waiting eagerly for him.

He did not go straight to the girl's office, but towards the passage ; it was so dark that it looked just a black void. He could not even make out the shape of doors against the wall. If there were light in any room, he would have seen it. He went along the carpeted floor —only the hall and staircase were without carpets—

using a pencil torch rather than switching on a light. Two doors showed up, and the staircase beyond. The doors probably led to the bedrooms ; the servants would sleep upstairs.

If he called out, he might disturb Blane or the servants ; the girl had been desperately anxious that he shouldn't do that. He went back towards the landing, disquiet much stronger now. Before, there had been puzzling features ; this stopped being puzzling, became inexplicable. He reminded himself again that he could be working up the atmosphere of alarm. Any moment, a door might open and the girl appear.

Nothing stirred.

He switched on the light of her room. It was over the desk, shaded so that the only bright light shone on to the desk, the rest of the room was gloomy. All the papers had been put away, there were a few oddments on it, and the portable typewriter now in its black case. The corner behind the door looked exactly as when he had left it, with the *Saturday Evening Post* lying there. He had pushed the door back against the wall, it had swung back slightly. He took no notice of that, but went to Blane's door. It was easy to imagine Blane sitting there, obese, breathless, the stick at hand—as easy to imagine his *tee-hee-hee*. Angry with himself, Mannering thrust the door open.

Darkness, broken by the faint glow from a fire that was nearly out, was beyond. Mannering stood for a few moments, to get used to the gloom. Furniture showed up ; the outline of chairs, the bookcases, even a faint reflection from the fire on the glass. He stared at the chair in which Blane had been sitting; and alarm began to creep through him.

He could see nothing above the back of the big chair; no head. But a foot showed near the kerb, just the front of a shoe, with a red glow on the polished cap. Then he was able to see more clearly—the first foot, the other, the legs, the rubber ferruled end of the walking stick, the white front of a shirt, the pale shape of face and hands.

Mannering felt for a light switch, found and pressed it, and clamped his teeth and turned to look at Blane.

It was a dead Blane. A fat hulk, slumped back in the chair, mouth slack, eyes slightly open as if he were looking through his lashes. The foot and top of a stocking, silk or nylon, hung over the front of his boiled shirt. Part of the knot showed beneath his chin. The rest of the stocking was buried in the flabby flesh, none of it was visible. The two plump hands lay on the arms of the chair, looking grotesquely as if he were still sleeping.

Dead ?

Mannering reached and touched him. His hands were still warm. The diamond ring sparkled. Could he have been like this when the girl had telephoned ? Could she have known ? Had she killed him, then called for Mannering with some wild thought that he would be able to help her ?

Or could she have sent for him, so that he might be found together with a dead Blane ?

He could hear Blane's breathless voice, as if echoing in his ear.

" *Go back to Jacob, tell him no. Not while I live.*"

The silence in the house was deathly.

Mannering pulled at the knotted stocking ; it was drawn tightly, wouldn't unfasten easily, might not unfasten at all without being cut. He felt the man's pulse ; there was no beat of life, he didn't think there was a chance of bringing life back.

One part of his mind told him that he ought to try ; the other cried a warning. He should get out of here, call the police and give Blane his chance that way. A patrol car would be here within five minutes ; probably less. He went forward to the telephone, which was near enough for Blane to reach without getting up. Fingerprints didn't matter, here was one case he wouldn't get involved in without keeping the police informed.

He lifted the receiver ; there was no sound, just a hollow deadness which came from a disconnected line. He rapped the platform up and down ; there was still no sound,

so it was useless to dial. Had it been cut ? He looked
at the cable leading from the wall installation, that seemed
all right. Forget it—the telephone was out of order, that
was that. He could get to another in a few minutes,
have the police here in time to do everything necessary
for Blane. He knew, deep down, that no one could do
anything for the fat man. He glanced at the parted lips
and partly open eyes again, and then swung round towards
the door—and stopped again, this time drenched with
a cold horror.

Blane wasn't alone.

Judy Darrow lay on the floor, as if dead.

*   *   *

It was like a picture in a foul dream. The girl lay awkwardly, her neck seemed to be twisted. The light gleamed
on her black braided hair.

The moment of horror passed.

Mannering went forward swiftly, and went down on one
knee beside her. Her neck was bruised and red. A
wide velvet neck-band with a cheap jewelled clasp had
twisted in the band, tightening it so that it choked her.
He tried to free it, failed, and took out a knife and cut
the band ; it fell slack. He tore it away.

He straightened the girl's body and knelt astride her,
pressing his hands against her ribs, not even knowing
whether there was life left, any chance that artificial respiration would bring her round.

He had to try.

He needed help, but if he waited for it, it would be too
late. Compared with her, Blane didn't matter. He began
to feel warm, reminded himself not to work too swiftly;
slow, regular pressure was the best. Was there a chance?

After five minutes, he was hot. He stopped, stood up,
took off his coat and jacket, dropped them on the floor
and began again. This time he didn't take count of time,
could think only of one thing—saving her life.

He stared down at her face, the slack lips—he was wasting
his time, she was as dead as Blane.

Why go on ?

Stop this, get out, call the police, start the hunt for the murderer ; only a fool would keep on trying. He watched her face with desperate anxiety for some sign that she was coming round, that he had fought death and beaten it. He began to give up hope, felt that he couldn't go on, the physical exertion was too great ; this ought to be done in relays. He would give her a better chance if he called the police ; they would take over, and have a doctor here within a few minutes. Why take this on himself ? Why——

Her lips *moved*.

It wasn't just the automatic movement with her body ; it was a movement which she herself made. He forgot tiredness, forgot the sweat which rimmed his eyes, beaded his forehead and his neck, forced himself to keep up the steady movement, and not to rush it. He stared at her face until sweat gathered on his eyelashes and he couldn't see clearly—but he saw the lips move again, and a movement in her throat.

Soon he knew that she would live.

This was the time to stop and send for the police. Find blankets, throw them over her to keep her warm, rush to a telephone and race back, so that he could start again, keeping up the respiration until help came. He *must* do that.

He couldn't go on himself any longer without a rest ; his knees, hands and shoulders ached, and pain kept streaking along his legs. He stood up unsteadily, dashed the sweat out of his eyes, made sure that Judy was breathing, then turned and moved towards the door ; he must get blankets from the bedroom, *must* keep her warm. By the time he had reached the passage he had more control of his movements. The first door was a bedroom, and he dragged blankets and an eiderdown off the bed and hurried back ; he was soaking with sweat.

He covered her, fought the temptation to go on working, turned and hurried to the head of the stairs. He wasn't too steady, must go carefully or would fall. He was giddy too. Crazy, that a little exertion should affect him like that. How long had he been working ? Much longer than he realised, perhaps, and putting every ounce of nervous energy into the task, knowing that he must save the girl. He could grin now—he had saved her. If someone started on her again within five minutes, she would be all right.

He wasn't sure.

He must call the neighbours and get them to telephone the police, then come back himself with one of them. He hoped they wouldn't be in too dead a sleep, it might take an age to wake them. He reached the front door, opened it and saw another light on the other side of the square ; so someone was awake, it needn't take long. He wanted to shout from here. He plunged out of the front door and on to the pavement—and kicked against something he hadn't seen.

He pitched forward, unable to save or to help himself. Instinctively he thrust his left shoulder forward, to take his weight on that ; the fall jolted him badly. He fell almost flat, but hadn't a moment's respite, hardly time to wonder what he had fallen over, before he felt hands touching him. He heard a muted voice, then felt fingers round his neck—cold fingers, which stung his hot skin. They did more. A flare of fear took hold of him as the thumb and fingers pressed, the thumbs in the back of his neck, the fingers in front, choking the breath out of him.

Fingers were strangling him—not a stocking.

He couldn't breathe, felt his head swimming, knew that he hadn't a chance if the man kept up the pressure.

CHAPTER V

WAKING

MANNERING was cold and stiff, something fell steadily and softly on his face and on his hands. It was dark.

Consciousness came back to him slowly, at first he had

no recollection of what had happened, there was only one question in his mind; what was falling on him? He moved his right arm and touched his face with his hand and realised that his fingers and cheeks were wet.

Was it rain?

He opened his eyes wider but there seemed to be no light at all, only greyness above and about him. The spots, for they were rain spots, fell against his eyes and he closed them quickly, tightly. He swallowed, and his throat hurt; he moved his left arm, and the shoulder was painful, as if it were badly bruised.

Then he began to remember.

It did not all come in one flash—the only blinding picture was of Judy Darrow, laying on the floor. That drove away thought and mind pictures of everything else, until the first shock was over; then the rest came back, while Mannering still lay face upwards. The stiffness at his shoulder had been caused by the fall; at his neck, pain came from the bruises caused by those tightening fingers and pressing thumbs.

Mannering turned over slowly, on to his right side, and began to get up. He was stiff all over, but only his neck and the one shoulder really hurt. He got to his knees, then unsteadily to his feet. The rain beat down on him with soft insistence. He could hear sounds, drops of water gathered on leaves and branches, dripping; somewhere not far off, they fell into a pool, and he could hear the steady splashing. The ground beneath his feet was soft and soggy—as wet grass might be.

He made out the shape of his arm—pale, because he had run out of 17 Maberley Square in his shirt-sleeves. Gradually, he made out the shapes of trees, black against the dark grey of the sky, but the clouds were so dark that he could not see any shape in them. He walked slowly forward, towards greyness which was not blocked by blackness; there was not likely to be anything in his way there. He took a dozen steps, and the stiffness began to wear off, he walked much more easily; but every time he swallowed, his neck hurt. He began to turn his head slowly, then put his fingers gingerly against his neck, and started massaging ; it caused more pain and seemed to ease nothing. He could turn his head towards the right more freely than to the left ; that way, a streak of pain shot from beneath his ear down his neck and to the top of his shoulder.

He kept walking, taking short strides in case something he couldn't see was in his path. Nothing stopped him. The first change came when his foot fell on a hard surface, and he realised that he was on a path. Now he began to wonder urgently where he was, and for the first time the urgency transcended the mental picture of the girl laying on the floor.

Was she alive ?

He refused to let himself think too much about her, forced the memory into the background and himself to worry about where he was. He still couldn't see, but took three steps and found himself on grass again ; the path, probably tarred, was little more than four feet wide. A path would lead to somewhere whichever way he went, it was safe to follow it.

Why was there no light at all ?

His mind wasn't working properly yet. There would be no light in any country district, there was no reason to think that he was still in London. He had no idea how long he had been unconscious. It had been after midnight when he had left the house, dawn did not come until nearly five o'clock ; it was somewhere between one o'clock and five, then.

He walked on more quickly, much less stiff but with his head held a little on one side, because of the pain at his neck. Lorna would ease that a lot by rubbing in embrocation ; there was nothing serious the matter with him, no one had intended to kill him.

Had they just meant to make sure that the girl died ?

It would be easy to fly into a panic about her. He had been much nearer panic than he had been for a long time, much nearer than he should. Had it simply been because of the girl ? Forget the why of it—where was he, when would he see light ?

He had no idea how long he walked before he saw a dozen little pin points of light in the distance. He realised that he had come out of the wooded land, that open ground stretched out in front of him, and not far away was a road lined with street lamps. There was something more ; a diffused light which grew brighter and then, above the soft patter of the rain the sound of a car. It drew level, and headlights swayed up and down ; then it passed and soon the lights disappeared, the car had turned a corner. Mannering doubted if it had been a mile away, and the path probably led straight to the road. He quickened his footsteps automatically, went too fast and stepped off the path on to soggy grass, and nearly fell.

At first the only discomfort which had mattered had been the painful stiffness ; now that from his sodden clothes was as bad. Rain dripped from his sleeves, ran down his face, over the backs of his hands.

It was not so dark as it had been.

In one direction he could make out a faint light in the sky. He felt his heart lift ; dawn was coming, that placed the time, and also told him that he was walking south-east. He could just make out the shining surface of the path, and as he went along, imagined that he could see the roofs of houses beyond the lighted road. The lamps were so much nearer that he could just make out the shape of the posts. It wouldn't be long before he could get to a telephone, a taxi, home, a hot bath, Lorna's soothing fingers and——

News of Judy Darrow.

Dread of what might have happened to her drove the other thoughts away, was almost an obsession which he had to fight. Then the headlights of another car came into view. He was within a hundred yards of the road, and began to run ; running wasn't easy. He waved his right arm and tried to shout, but his voice was a croak and shouting hurt so much that he stopped trying. The

car swished by, not fifty yards away, and he stood still and
watched it disappear round the corner, feeling vicious
towards the unwitting driver.

The obsession had faded. As he reached the road,
Mannering found himself grinning at the rage he had
felt for the man who could not have seen him. If another
car approached he would step into the middle of the road
to stop it. Or would it be wiser to go to one of the houses,
across the road ? These were large, and stood in their
own grounds, he could see that ; he could also see the
trees in most of the gardens. There was no bright light
except that from the street lamps, but the dawn was
bringing its reluctant glow and he could see the branches
of the trees, shrubs, the glistening road and pavements
on either side. Everything had a vaguely familiar look,
he felt that he had been here before. That teased him.

Both cars had been travelling left ; he turned left for
no other reason. The water squelched from his shoes,
his trousers clung to his legs, and his waistcoat and shirt
to his back. He had never felt more uncomfortable,
but movement had warmed him a little, and the pain was
less acute except in his throat whenever he swallowed.
He fought against swallowing ; and whenever he had to,
it brought a bigger effort and greater pain.

What was that pain, compared with the girl's ?

Was she dead ?

No other car came. The houses looked blank and
empty. They weren't, he ought to go and knock someone up ; servants would soon be stirring. He would
have crossed the road but for the sight of crossroads nearby ;
telephone kiosks were often installed at crossroads. He
hurried again, and as he drew nearer them he saw a street
lamp shining on the red and grey of a kiosk. He slid his
left hand into his pocket, reminding himself that his
shoulder could still hurt. No one had robbed him—he
had his coppers in that pocket and could feel the weight
of silver in the other, his keys, a small wallet and oddments
in his hip pocket. He took out three pennies, judging
from the touch of them, reached the telephone kiosk and

leaned against it for moments that seemed long. Once inside, he could call Lorna and bring the warmth that he needed, put an end to this nightmare—but he wouldn't be able to find out whether Judy was alive.

She and Blane might be in that library, cold and stiff with *rigor mortis*, the fire dead and the ashes grey, nothing reflecting from the glass of the bookcases.

He pulled open the heavy door of the kiosk and squeezed himself in. He hadn't as much strength as a kitten; the door fell against the back of his leg, and he winced. Trifling hurts worried him. He put the pennies, one by one, on top of the prepayment box, and looked at the little disc in front of the telephone. It said, *Wimbledon* 34143.

So the road was familiar. He had been on Wimbledon Common, was now on the Merton Road. Putney was down the hill, London just beyond. There would be plenty of all night garages there, he could call for a taxi; or have Lorna call for one. He needn't go any further than the crossroads, it was a good place for the cabby to find him. He found himself smiling faintly, lifted the receiver, put two pennies in the slot—and nudged the third off. It fell to the cement floor with a clear ringing sound.

Clumsy fool!

There was little room in here. Mannering looked down but couldn't see the penny, only his feet and the muddy marks he had made. He turned slowly, able to see clearly from the light that had gone on when he had come inside, but he didn't see the penny. He backed against the door, opening it a little, and the thing was still out of sight. He backed out, holding the door open with his leg, looked everywhere, and saw it in a corner which was difficult to get at. He had to get it, there had been just three pennies in his pocket; he always kept enough to make a telephone call.

He moved his leg, the door banged against the side of his head. It made his head ring and jolted his neck, a streak of pain made him wince again. What was the matter with him? Why couldn't he get a grip on himself?

He went down on one knee, groped along the floor and touched the penny. He couldn't pick it up easily, the head of Queen Victoria as a girl was face uppermost—the thing must be nearly a hundred years old, and was worn as flat as copper could be. Why the devil didn't they take pennies like that out of circulation? He prised it up with his nail, got it between his fingers, and held it tightly; he couldn't bear going through that again. He felt like a village idiot as he put it carefully into the slot; it fell through, safely.

Now he could dial.

F L A 83451. There was an extension of the telephone in the bedroom, it would soon wake Lorna. Wake her? Would she have slept? She was a light sleeper, and knowing he was out, she would probably keep waking, hoping to hear him. By now she would be in a state of alarm not far from panic. A family failing, today.

The ringing sound started. *Brrr-brrr : brrr-brrr.* Any moment he would hear her voice, it wouldn't be sleepy but alert with eagerness overcoming anxiety. *Brrr-brrr : brrr-brrr.* Any moment now—she might be in the kitchen, making a cup of tea. The telephones were in the study, drawing-room and bedroom. *Brrr-brrr.* It always seemed a long time, when one felt miserable and uncomfortable. There was no reason for anxiety, she would soon answer. *Brrr-brrr : brrr-brrr.*

This didn't just seem a long time; it was. There was no answer, and that didn't make sense. Had he got a wrong number? The dial telephones let one down sometimes, or he might have slipped up. He pressed Button B to get his pennies back, took them out of the little cup one by one, inserted them into the slot again, and dialled afresh; he didn't make any mistake this time.

Brrr-brrr : brrr-brrr.

There was no answer. He stood with the receiver to his ear for several minutes, and had to accept the fact that Lorna wasn't there. He pressed Button B and got his pennies back. Why no answer, just after five in the morning ? She would have been alarmed, but would she go anywhere to look for him ? Would she go——

To Maberley Square, of course, she knew where he had gone. He'd better call Blane's house. At least, if Lorna had gone there she would have found Blane, might have arrived in time to give Judy a chance, but what would her thoughts be like ? Her mind would be absolute turmoil, she would be tormented by the possibility that he had run into desperate trouble.

He had memorised Blane's address but didn't know the telephone number. The thick London Directory, in its four sections, was lodged in the cubby hole beneath the telephone. He pulled out the top one ; the first volume, A to E, was at the bottom. He dropped one taking this out, then thumbed over the pages, found the BL's, and then Blane, W, 17, Maberley Square, Mayfair 22551. He dialled very carefully, and the familiar ringing sound didn't come.

The line had been out of order ; but if the police had arrived, surely they would have put it right by now ? He tried again, with the same result. Now he was beginning to shiver, partly with cold, partly with annoyance.

His mind just wasn't working ; why hadn't he called Scotland Yard, or dialled 999 ? He didn't know why, got the pennies back again and hesitated before he decided on either number, changed his mind and tried the flat again. *Brrr-brrr : brrr-brrr.*

" Hallo ? " It was Lorna, he'd nothing more to worry about ! " *Hallo ?* "

" Hallo, my sweet," said Mannering, and knew that his voice didn't sound normal ; speaking hurt. " Sorry I'm——"

" John," she said. It wasn't just with relief, there was much more than that in her tone. " John, is it you ? I don't recognise your voice. Never mind. I've just arrived here with Bristow. Don't come back, yet, stay away. I'll tell you more——"

What madness was this ?

Mannering heard a man's voice in the background, but couldn't catch the words. He heard Lorna's sharp : " I shall not ! " Then she spoke into the telephone again. " John, Blane was found murdered, there was a robbery. Jewels. Bristow is here, he knows you were at the house. Bristow wants you. He——"

She broke off.

Mannering forgot his cold misery.

Bristow knew he had been the Baron, Bristow had never been convinced that the Baron's old habits had gone for good. Any policeman would suspect him, would have to take action. Mannering had to accept not only that but the fact that Lorna was shaken out of her habitual calmness. Bristow had frightened her enough to make her warn Mannering that if he went home he would walk into danger; obviously the degree of that danger terrified her. She was shocked, not quite herself; that didn't mean she was wrong.

" He's going to speak to you," Lorna said quickly. " Be careful what you say."

A moment later, Mannering heard Bristow's clear voice.

CHAPTER VI

ANGRY DETECTIVE

AT any other time Bristow's would be a good voice to hear. It wasn't good now, but hard—even the tone seemed to accuse, to confirm all that Lorna had implied.

" What the hell are you up to, Mannering ? "

Bristow was a friend most of the time but there was no friendliness. There hadn't been with Lorna, or she wouldn't have talked as she had. She was distraught, or she would have told him to come back and fight this out ; Mannering couldn't get that out of his mind.

If he went back there'd be plenty of questions to answer ; the police would hold him, perhaps for days. He could tell his story but not make them believe it. Blane, defending himself, could have made those bruises on Mannering's neck; the others could have come from a fall anywhere.

Above everything, Mannering needed time to think; and to be free while thinking.

" Are you there ? " Bristow barked.

Bristow wouldn't believe him capable of murder ; but Bristow might believe that Blane had caught him burgling the house, and been killed in a frenzied struggle. Lorna was convinced that Bristow's thoughts ran on those lines, that danger was acute.

" Mannering, are you there ? " Bristow couldn't keep the anger out of his voice.

Mannering found calmness easier than he'd expected.

" Yes, Bill, what's eating you ? "

" Speak up ! "

Mannering put his lips closer to the mouthpiece.

" What's all this about ? Why bellow at me ? "

" Where are you ? I want to see you ! " The Yard man's voice was a little less harsh. Occasionally when Bristow lost his temper he said more than he should; this time he simply declared that he was hostile—much more than hostile. He must have shown that to Lorna, so scaring her into advising Mannering to keep away. Being Bristow, he might have meant to do that—to give the Baron a chance to see the situation clearly. Mannering had never needed a clearer mind, never been in a worse condition to make sure of having one.

" Bill, what's got under your skin ? "

" You know. Listen, Mannering, it won't help you to keep away from me. Not this time. We know everything. My God, what in hell possessed *you* to do it ? I——"

Lorna said something ; her words weren't clear, but she sounded shrill. The telephone made strange noises, almost as if she were struggling to get it away from Bristow. Mannering stood stiffly in front of the telephone, listening, growing more tense. Then Bristow came on the line again.

" Tell me where you are, Mannering, and wait there—I'll send for you. I've got to hear your story. So far I'm the only one who knows it was you, understand ? I've got to know your story before I do anything else but I can't wait much longer. Where are you ? "

He was showing belated caution.

Mannering said slowly and heavily :

" Never mind, Bill, I don't like you in this mood."

He rang off, and as he took his hands away from the receiver he knew he had committed himself to a lot of trouble. He could have found logical reasons for letting Bristow send for him, but Bristow's mood and Lorna's manner had made it clear that he'd be in Queer Street. The way out wasn't *via* a remand cell. A lot had happened that Mannering didn't know about, yet. Only one thing stood out, and he accepted it in spite of its apparent nonsense; he was under suspicion for Blane's murder, and perhaps for the girl's.

Was Judy dead ?

As Mannering, as the owner of Quinns, Mannering might have taken the chance and waited for Bristow's men ; but he was more than that. He was the man who had been in danger from the police so often that it had once been a constant menace. The years of the Baron had planted wariness of the law so deeply in his mind that whenever crisis came he would intuitively trust his wits to keep him out of trouble, to fend off the police until he knew both his strength and weakness.

He stepped out of the kiosk. There were others he could call, for help—others who would give it, too—but he had no change small enough for the telephone. The calls would probably be a waste of time, anyhow ; if he called Larraby or Carruthers, he would almost certainly find that the police were with them.

Would he ?

Bristow had said that he was the only one who knew the whole story—but Bristow wouldn't take serious chances and would have Mannering's contacts watched without telling anyone why. He could try later, but it probably wouldn't get him anywhere. A man named Sol, an old Jew with a theatrical make-up shop in the Edgware Road, might be his best bet. There were ways he could help himself. He had a car in a lock-up garage which no one knew was his, there had been other emergencies when the Baron had become that substantial ghost, and he had never dropped precautions. In the car was enough money to tide him over for a few days. Once he felt better, he would be able to laugh at this, get a kick out of a battle of wits.

Laugh ?

Was that girl dead ?

A cyclist came along the road from Putney Hill, looking at Mannering intently. It was still raining ; no wonder the cyclist stared as if he couldn't believe his eyes at a man in his shirtsleeves who had obviously been out all night. Two cars came behind the cyclist, the first of the morning traffic. It was almost broad daylight now, must be nearly six o'clock.

Cyclists and cars passed.

Mannering thought of a dozen things that he ought to do. The first was to make himself take this calmly, make sure that every step was the right one. First, he needed a coat ; then a hot drink ; he should concentrate on those. There were cafés in Putney, one or two would probably be open early—he was less than a mile from a main road where traffic would already be fairly thick. He glanced along the road behind him and his first slice of luck came in sight—a big red bus, travelling fast, the first of the morning on that route. Mannering was close to a bus stop. The driver, the conductor with a big nose and several passengers downstairs looked at him with as much astonishment as the cyclist. Bristow might get on to them later in the morning, but it wasn't yet desperately urgent to hide all his traces.

He tendered half a crown.

" Save you coming up," he said. " Do you know

of a restaurant open for breakfast ? " He forced a smile, made a fair job at speaking normally.

" One at the bottom of the hill, along Wandsworth Road, give you a good square meal there." The big nose twitched.

" Thanks," said Mannering. He went to the top deck, there was an empty seat right at the back, few people were likely to notice him and none likely to stare. He began to shiver, but they were soon at the top of Putney Hill, and stopped only three times before Mannering got off where the conductor had told him. That was within sight of Putney Bridge; the Thames was hidden by the rain which had become little more than a drizzle. Everyone on the bus stared after him.

Three lorry drivers were in the café, and a middle-aged man behind the desk.

Mannering left half an hour afterwards, warmer, dry, wearing an old suit and a cap bought from the café owner for two pounds, adequately fed, his stiffness much better except at his neck and left shoulder. The story of a break-down with his car had satisfied the owner, but now a dozen or more people who had seen him that morning would recognise him from a photograph.

He had to do what the Baron had so often done—go to earth. From the moment he had hung up on Bristow, there would have been a call out for him. Practically every policeman, certainly every man of the Criminal Investigation Department, and far too many members of the general public would recognise him. His shapeless clothes and the peaked cloth cap would give him a brief respite ; that wouldn't last.

Should he try old Sol ?

There was a telephone kiosk near the café, and he now had plenty of coppers. He listened to the ringing sound again, and it carried his mind back to the ordeal by waiting at the other telephone—and the crazy reason for what had followed. He didn't know everything about it, but he knew it was crazy.

An old man answered.

" Thith iss Sol speaking."

" Hallo, Sol," Mannering said. His voice was nearer normal, except that it was painful when he used it. " This is John Mannering. I——"

" Mithter Mannering." The old man interrupted and his voice was pitched low, his tone gave him away as much as Bristow's. " Pleath don't come here, pleath don't, for your own sake."

" So Bristow's seen you," Mannering said heavily.

" He sent a man, yeth, not ten minutes ago. I am to report if you call me, I shall not, Mithter Mannering, Brithtow knows that, there is an officer watching. Mithter Mannering, I don't know what all the trouble is about but I want to help you—you can hear me ? "

" Go on," Mannering said.

" Be patient, and remember thith number, Mithter Mannering. Whitechapel 21223. That is easy—thay it, pleath."

" Whitechapel 21223." Mannering's voice was less tense.

" In real emergency, call there, but not until after tonight, not before eleven o'clock tonight. I will try to have some arrangements made. You underthtand, don't you, Mr. Mannering ? "

" Yes, Sol. And thanks."

" After you have done tho much for me in the patht ? No thanks, pleath, Mr. Mannering ! For the day, be careful, very careful. Brithtow also telephoned, he is an angry man. Be very careful of angry friends, Mr. Mannering."

" All right, Sol."

Mannering rang off, stepped out of the kiosk, glanced up and down, and saw a policeman strolling along the other side of the street. The policeman had already seen him, could have recognised him even at a distance of fifty yards. He turned his back on the man but didn't hurry. He stopped by a tobacconist and newspaper shop, took a paper and dropped the coppers into a cardboard box —and glanced towards the constable, who wasn't hurrying.

This was the real beginning ; and Sol had told him how swiftly the police were acting.

Mannering went back, passed the policeman on the other side of the road, and didn't earn a second glance. A bus ran from Putney High Street to Victoria Station, near the lock-up garage. He stood with a dozen others in a queue, and no one glanced at him twice. He opened his newspaper, read the headlines and then looked for the *stop press*. He felt as if everyone in sight were watching him. He read.

Wealthy Man Strangled

William Blane, wealthy owner of 17 Maberley Square found strangled early this morning. His secretary Miss Judy Darrow narrowly escaped similar death. Miss Darrow is in nursing home, suffering from shock and minor injuries. Scotland Yard is anxious to interview anyone seen about midnight in neighbourhood of Maberley Square, Mayfair.

A bus came up. A man who had joined the queue behind Mannering pushed against him and muttered something. Mannering saw that most of the people were already on the bus, and hurried. He went upstairs, with one sentence echoing in his mind. ' His secretary, Miss Judy Darrow, narrowly escaped similar death '. So that effort had been worth while, shock and minor injuries probably meant little. He found himself smiling freely for the first time that morning.

He didn't smile much on the way to Victoria. In Chelsea, the bus filled up, a fat man sat next to him with a newspaper spread out ; a short fat man, not so fat as Blane but fat enough to remind Mannering of Blane in that easy chair with the foot and end of the stocking dangling on his chest.

Victoria seemed full of policemen ; none took any special notice of Mannering. The lock-up garages were in a side street—he had chosen them because they faced a warehouse wall and the side street was seldom used ; only the other people who garaged their cars in the other

three garages were ever about. No one was there, then.
His garage was Number 1 ; and his assailants had left him
his keys. There was a window, light, a change of clothes,
everything—well, most things—he would need. He hadn't
decided what to do next. This was sanctuary, and he would
feel easy in his mind here, plan the next step carefully.
If he wanted to, he could use make-up and change his
appearance—but there were risks in that.

He turned the key in the lock, but didn't open the door,
for a man passed the end of the street. Once the footsteps
had faded, Mannering opened the door, pulling it towards
him. As he pulled it and daylight shone on the Buick
inside, he saw a man getting out of the car.

CHAPTER VII

NEWS FROM JOSH LARRABY

THE bad moment passed. The man getting out of the
car had curly grey hair, a chubby face which made many
look at him twice and often gave Lorna the urge to paint
him. This was Josh Larraby. His grey eyes were heavy
with sleep, and he looked apologetic as he stood by the
side of the car, and Mannering closed the garage door.
Light came through the frosted windows.

" Hallo, Josh," greeted Mannering dryly. " Next
time I'll probably die of fright."

" Or hit me over the head and ask questions afterwards," Larraby said in a gentle voice ; there was gentle-
ness above everything else in the man, who was nearly
a head shorter than Mannering. " I'm really sorry,
I——"

" Dropped off. How long have you been here ? "

" Since about three o'clock."

" What happened ? " Mannering asked.

" It began when Mrs. Mannering looked out of her

window and saw a man following you when you left Chelsea," Larraby said. "She gave you time to get to Maberley Square, then rang up to warn you, but there was no reply. The exchange said the line was out of order. She telephoned me at the shop a little before half past one, and asked me to meet her at Maberley Square."

"Go on," said Mannering softly.

"The door was unlatched, and we went up and found— Blane dead. Then Mrs. Mannering found the girl coming round on her bed. I kept out of the room."

"What did the girl say?"

"She said she'd caught you with your hands round Blane's neck," Larraby said, quietly.

Mannering felt as if he'd been kicked; he didn't speak.

"She also said that you turned on her, and that she thought that she was going to die."

"Judy Darrow is a nice young woman," said Mannering very softly. "What else did she say?"

"She had asked you to go and see her and had told you that the door would be unlocked. She didn't hear you come, but heard a noise in the man's room, and found you there."

"Killing him with my hands?"

Josh nodded. "That's what she said, but there was a stocking round the man's neck."

"Even if someone cut the stocking away after I left the police would have known one had been used," Mannering said; that was a measure of his reluctance to believe that there was more than circumstantial evidence against him. "How was the girl dressed?" Details mattered, not because he could learn anything from them now, but because he might later.

"Dressed?" echoed Larraby.

"*Was* she dressed, or in pyjamas?"

"Oh, yes. I saw her only through the crack of the door," Larraby said, frowning. "I *think* she wore a jumper and skirt. Yes, that's it, a yellow jumper and a black skirt. Her feet were bare, I remember. She told Mrs. Mannering

that she was going to send for the police, and felt faint—
she seemed in a daze."

Larraby could see the girl in her canary yellow jumper
and not be sure at first what she was wearing. Josh had
a two-track mind—for the Mannerings and for precious
stones. Forget that. Lorna had found Judy coming
round, in a different room. Mannering doubted if the
girl could have recovered enough to move by herself ;
someone must have finished the work he had started,
given her a stimulant, put her on her feet again, and—told
her what to say ? That might be the answer to the main
question. But why had she done it ? From malice
towards him? She didn't know him, had no possible cause
for malice. She owed her life to him, even if she didn't know
it; seldom had Mannering worked with such desperation.

He found himself lighting a cigarette.

" Did she know you were there ? "

" No. Mrs. Mannering left her to come and talk to
me. She was terribly worried. She told me where to
get this key, and to come and wait here, in case you came."
Never before had anyone but the Mannerings known
about this hide-out. " I was awake till after five. I
hope you've telephoned her ? "

" Bristow was with her," Mannering said, and Larraby
drew a sharp breath.

" That's very bad. But he can't believe you did this."

" He could, at a pinch," said Mannering feelingly.
" Or he might want us to think he believes it. He knows
I was there, of course, my prints must be all over the
place. I suppose he found the car outside, too. But
Bristow doesn't usually jump his fences at the first bit of
circumstantial evidence."

" It's more than circumstantial," Larraby said, and
rubbed his chin. His manner as well as his words increased
Mannering's anxiety, brought tension back. Coming on
top of Lorna's warning and Bristow's harshness, it was
frightening. Larraby meant it to be ; meant to make
sure that Mannering didn't take anything too lightly.
" Your car wasn't there when we arrived."

"Well, well," said Mannering woodenly. "Who sent for the police ? "

"Oh, the girl. She kept saying that she must. Mrs. Mannering delayed her as long as she could, short of forcing her not to."

There had been nothing else for Lorna to do.

"Did the police see you ? "

"No. I got away just before they arrived. But Bristow can easily find out that I was out most of the night ; if he does, he'll guess why."

Mannering said : "Yes, I suppose so," and drew hard on his cigarette, then dropped it on the cement floor and trod it out. "What time did the police arrive ? "

"About half past two."

"And Bristow was fooled by the little miss," said Mannering. Feeling vicious didn't help ; but he felt vicious.

"She made it sound very convincing even when she told Mrs. Mannering," Larraby said.

If you were a policeman, you had to accept evidence, had to act on it without being influenced by your own opinions. Bristow might find it hard to believe that Mannering had strangled Blane, but had been forced to act on the girl's statement. It was becoming easier to understand Bristow ; his anger would stem partly from disbelief, partly from the fact that it almost looked as if a man for whom he had respect and liking had had a brainstorm.

Mannering began to smile.

"Believe it, Josh ? "

Larraby raised his right hand, gave an answering smile, and seemed to relax.

"You don't really need to ask, Mr. Mannering. It isn't true, but I have a strong feeling that it is going to be difficult to make the girl retract. If she maintains the story the police will have to think of it in conjunction with your finger prints and the certainty that you were there— and that the jewels were gone."

"Ah, yes," said Mannering. "The jewels. Know anything about them ? "

" There were the rubies you wanted to buy from Blane,"
Larraby said ; it was almost inevitable. " I don't know
whether anything else was gone. The safe had been
forced and the jewels taken. The girl told Mrs. Mannering
—she didn't know who Mrs. Mannering was, then—that
you'd seen Blane this afternoon, and offered to buy the
rubies. The Korra rubies, I think she called them."

" Korra," echoed Mannering. " Josh, your main job—
try to find something about a Jacob Korra. Try every
way you know."

" I will."

" Fine. Do you know where the safe was ? "

" In the room where the dead man sat."

" You didn't see it ? "

" Yes, it was built into the wall behind a lower section
of one of the bookcases. That was the only thing that
really upset Mrs. Mannering, she was—well, you can imagine
how she behaved, she was magnificent. But the fact that
you——"

" I'd what ? " Mannering asked softly.

Larraby hesitated, then said firmly : " The fact that
you had opened the safe and taken the jewels really upset
her."

" I suppose it would," conceded Mannering. He was
smiling again, and not because he was amused. This
was a brilliant job ; no one could have framed him more
cunningly had they set out to do just that. Bristow's
reason might reject the possibility that Mannering had
killed Blane, but would readily believe that the Baron
had forced the safe and taken the jewels. Bristow proved
time and time again that he had never been wholly convinced
that the Baron was dead ; had a healthy respect for that
ghost. There was a mind behind this murder which
Mannering began to respect. " Yes, it would upset her,
Josh. Tell her I didn't, will you ? "

" You didn't *take* them ? " Even Josh found that hard
to believe.

Mannering said easily : " Cross my heart, Josh ! "
He felt more himself, had absorbed the shocks and could

begin to think clearly. " Tell Mrs. Mannering that,
and tell her I've something to look for." For the first
time since he had come round, he saw things to do that
might help to untangle all this. " And this is vital. She is
to telephone Daniel Farley at his private address, as soon
as she can—she'll find the number in the folder in the study.
She's to tell Farley what's happened, and ask him to act
for me. Understand, Josh ? Farley's to act for me."

" Your own solicitor——"

" This time it has to be Farley. It will put the seal
of professional confidence on him, and I don't want him
to tell the police any of the people he told me about. It's
the first job."

" I'll telephone——"

" No, talk to Mrs. Mannering," said Mannering,
" Bristow's probably got the line tapped by now. Did
you bring anything with you ? "

" Mrs. Mannering gave me seven pounds, all the money
she had with her, and I had nine." Larraby was apologetic. " There wasn't time to get anything else, clothes or
food."

" I'm luckier than you, I've had breakfast ! Everything
I'm likely to need is here, too, except somewhere to lie
low for a bit. Any ideas, Josh ? "

" That shouldn't give us much trouble," Larraby said
promptly. " I have a friend who will make you comfortable and say nothing, even if she suspects who you
are." He took a pencil from his pocket and scribbled on
a small pad, tore the sheet off and handed it to Mannering.
" Just tell her I sent you and will be seeing her, Mr. Mannering. I'll arrange for her to let you have more money,
if you need it, too. It's quite central, in St. John's Wood."

" Wonderful. Is there a garage ? "

" No, but plenty of room to stand the car in the drive."

" Couldn't be better," said Mannering. " Use the
address for messages, and contact it by telephone as often
as you can, in case I've something to pass on. Tell Mrs.
Mannering not to worry, this can't last long. Find Jacob
Korra—his past and his present. All right ? "

" Is there nothing else you need ? "

" Not yet," said Mannering. " You'd better slip out now, you might be recognised even if I'm not when I drive off. Thanks, Josh."

" Mr. Mannering." Larraby was earnest.

" Yes."

" Don't take this too lightly, will you ? I heard the way that girl talked to Mrs. Mannering, and if she spoke to the police in the same way, then they are almost certainly convinced that you did kill Blane. They're probably sure that you took the rubies, too. It would be hard to think of a more awkward situation."

Awkward was one word.

" I'll be careful," Mannering said, and chuckled—as if the last thing in the world he would be was careful. " It should be exciting while it lasts. Don't forget to tell Mrs. Mannering the importance of briefing Farley, and——"

He stopped abruptly.

He wanted Farley's lips sealed in professional confidence to prevent the police from learning too soon about Lady Jane Creswell and Aristotle Wynne ; but both names and addresses were in the file folder in the study. Bristow had probably searched the flat for the rubies, might already know of both people.

" Josh, that folder I mentioned—if Bristow hasn't seen it, burn it. I don't want him to know where I'm likely to be. Telephone this place in St. John's Wood about the folder, I need to know what's happened to it. Hurry."

CHAPTER VIII

FIRST MESSAGE

THE house in St. John's Wood, 15 Meybrick Road, was at the end of a street of small, narrow houses, mostly in

need of new paint. In the front room window was a
printed card, reading *Apartments*. Larraby knew what
he was about, but the card had given Mannering his first
doubt about the sanctuary; the landlady might not talk,
other boarders might. He wanted a place where he could
go in and out freely, where no one could get a close look
at him.

If he kept to his room, it should be all right.

He rang the bell, heard footsteps immediately, and a
big, hardy-looking woman wearing a blue smock, iron
grey hair cut in a bob and hanging straight from a centre
parting, opened the door. She had small bright blue eyes
which seemed to reflect the sky—and certainly missed
nothing.

" 'Morning." She was brisk.

" I think you know Josh Larraby, Mrs. Webber,"
Mannering said.

She gave more beam than smile, and brought dimples
to fat cheeks which were pale but not flabby.

" I should think I do know Josh! Didn't I look after
him like a mother for years ? " She stood aside, reassuringly, and looked as if she knew exactly what she was
about. " Come in, don't stand on the doorstep. How
is Josh ? Last time I saw him, he was almost a millionaire—
got a new job and being paid double what he was worth.
That's what he *said*." She thrust open the door of a room
on the right of the narrow passage; it was just a big room,
furnished with several big armchairs, a Victorian sofa, a
carpet of hideous modern design and an upright piano.
" Seen him lately ? "

" An hour or so ago. He said that if he vouched for
me, you would take no notice of anything you read in
the newspapers." Mannering found himself smiling; the
woman had a zest for life which wouldn't be easily damped.

Her eyes widened.

" Like *that*, is it ? Well, Josh wouldn't let me down,
mister. I think I'd sooner trust him than anyone else I
know. What have you been up to ? " Her eyes glowed
at him.

Mannering kept a straight face.

" Getting myself suspected of murder."

" Murder," she echoed, and the twinkle faded. But she would know about it as soon as the late morning papers arrived ; at the latest, when the evening papers came. Mannering had rejected the thought of using full disguise while here, it would be too much of a strain to act a part both here and when he was out of the house. At the garage he had used grease-paint sparingly, slipped rubber cheek-pads into his mouth ; he had the make-up box from the Buick with him.

" That's nasty, mister," Mrs. Webber said heavily.

" I don't like it much myself."

The twinkle began to come back.

" Well, we'll see," she said. " I expect Josh will tele-phone me—and if I don't think you ought to stay, I'll give you plenty of time to get somewhere else. Never did have much time for the police myself. The first time they put my old man inside, it was for something he never did. I'll *never* believe he did it, but he made his mistakes afterwards. They never gave him a chance." She didn't speak bitterly, but as if her ' old man ' was no longer with her. " I'd better know your name," she said, " any name will do, if you're nervous."

" Mannering."

She moved back a pace.

" *Mannering ?* "

" Yes."

" But that's the name of Josh's boss ! "

" Josh works for me."

" Streuth," said Mrs. Webber, gustily, " I never expected to be looking after a real gent. Can't tell what's going to happen from one day to the next, can you ? " She took a few seconds to get used to the identity of her new boarder. " Well, my food's all right—I'm just a plain cook, mind you—and I'm *clean*. Look at all the linen, even behind the piano—I move that out every week of my life. Had breakfast ? "

" Yes, but I'd like a cup of tea."

" Kettle's on, it's always on in this house," announced
Mrs. Webber. " I'd better take you up to your room.
Want to have your meals up there, I suppose. Needn't
worry about the other boarders, I've only got two, both
leave the house before half past seven in the morning,
back soon after six, and then usually out again by seven.
Just lie low when they're in, that's all. I'll show you."
She led the way out of the room and up the stairs, which
were narrow and carpeted with a plain-coloured matting.
" Better give you the room on the top floor. Got a bath,
everything you'll want, but the second flight of steps is
pretty steep."

" It sounds just right."

It was, for this emergency; a large room overlooking
the street, with a huge double bed against one wall, a single
bed in another corner. Two rugs were by the side of the
bed, covering the worn linoleum. There were two com-
fortable-looking easy chairs, oddments of furniture, a
bedside light and, just across the passage, a bathroom with
' everything '.

" Okay ? "

" Fine ! "

" Fancy you being that John Mannering," marvelled
Mrs. Webber. " Often read about you in the papers,
took a kind of personal interest since Josh started to work
for you. I don't mind saying that anyone who would
give a position of *trust* after Josh made *his* mistake goes
up in my estimation. If people would only judge from
the man himself, not what he's done in the past, there'd
be a lot less trouble. Josh met my old man inside, that's
how he come to get acquainted. Lumme, hark at me, and
you gasping for a cuppa. There's a gas ring, see, after
this you can make your own. Won't be long."

She closed the door on him firmly.

Mannering went to the window, opened it and looked
out ; the drop to the front garden was sheer, there was
no drain pipe within reach, no way of getting down. He
went across to the bathroom ; that window overlooked a
narrow garden, a pipe and window-ledges which would

enable him to climb down in a hurry, if there were an emergency. He looked into the third room on this floor. It was full of trunks, cases, old furniture, rolls of linoleum and oddments. He went back into the bathroom, where there was a hatch to the loft, stood on a stool, moved the hatch to one side, and hauled himself up. Water gurgled in a cistern, the only light came from a tiny window—there was no easy way out through the roof.

He dropped down again, pulled the hatch cover into position, washed his hands and went back to the bedroom. Mrs. Webber wasn't on her way upstairs. Mrs. Webber *might* go for the police, after seeing the morning news-papers. He didn't think it likely, and Josh felt sure she wouldn't; but Josh had no idea how she would react if she came to the conclusion that she was shielding a murderer.

Now that he had taken the plunge, doubts about its wisdom flooded over Mannering. Apart from the few minutes while talking with the woman, he had been glum and pessimistic—because Bristow might already know about Lady Jane Creswell and Aristotle Wynne. The girl had heard the names on the dictaphone record.

He heard Mrs. Webber coming up, climbing quickly but putting a lot of weight on every stair. He opened the door, and she came in with a large tray on which was a pot of tea, a tin of biscuits, bowl of sugar and a jug of milk ; a tin kettle hung from the fat little finger of her left hand. Under her arm was a newspaper.

He took the tray from her, put it on the table near the gas fire and the gas ring.

" Ta," she said. " You've got yourself into a *proper* mess, haven't you ? "

" Let's just say I'm in one." Her forthrightness eased his gloom again, and her eyes were as bright blue up here as they had been at the front door. " What does the paper say ? "

" Well it doesn't say you killed the man and tried to kill the girl, but I can read between the lines," said Mrs. Webber. She looked at him intently. " The picture flatters you," she said, and handed him the *Daily Cry*.

" If you ask me, you've done something to your face."

" A little."

" Get rid of that moustache and no one will recognise you," went on Mrs. Webber. " Your wife's *lovely*, isn't she ? "

Mannering didn't answer, but studied the front page. His photograph and Lorna's were there, studio portraits which did him more than justice, Lorna less. The story of the murder began with the simple facts, followed with an almost sinister :

" The police are anxious to interview Mr. John Mannering, famed as a connoisseur of jewels, one-time consultant to Scotland Yard, who they think may be able to give them valuable information."

That was the old formula, and hadn't fooled Mrs. Webber ; it would fool no one. Mannering looked for mention of his car and saw none. Judy Darrow's story wasn't quoted, and her photograph wasn't there. One of a man with the caption: *William Blane, the murdered man*, showed a plump face but gave no indication of Blane's excessive fat ; so he hadn't always been fat.

Somewhere, far off, a bell rang.

" *Damn !* " exclaimed Mrs. Webber. " Sure as I ever climb those stairs, that blasted bell has to ring. It's the telephone. If it's for you, I'll just shout, so leave the door open."

She hurried off ; and Mannering waited at the head of the stairs, but she didn't call him.

He went back, drank his tea, went into the bathroom and cut his moustache as close as he could, then shaved. He brought the make-up case from the bedroom, patched up the grease-paint at his eyes, made a few other lines which altered the general look of his face. All the time he strained his ears to catch the sound of the telephone bell. Larraby could have finished doing everything he'd been asked now ; but might have difficulty in getting away from the police to call him. So might Lorna. They wouldn't call from the flat or from the shop. Larraby's home telephone number might be tapped, too. They would have to use a public telephone, and if Bristow were really putting on the pressure, they would probably be followed wherever they went. Larraby might already be in trouble because he had been out ; might be at the Yard, being questioned, might not have had a chance to get that message to Lorna. Mannering had told him not to telephone, but a telephone call might have been his only chance of sending word.

Until Farley had been briefed for him, and he knew what had happened to that file, Mannering could not safely make a move.

He was half-way between the bathroom and the bedroom when he heard Mrs. Webber call—a single, stentorian:

" *Telephone !* "

He hurried down the stairs, was at the first landing when he paused. He could trust her too much. She had only to call him and bring him running down—to find the police waiting. It was always like this ; he'd taken too big a chance on Larraby's recommendation.

Mrs. Webber stood at the foot of the lower flight of stairs.

" Just along here," she said, and pointed along the passage which ran by the stairs. " It's Josh."

Fears faded.

The telephone stood on a ledge in a recess behind the staircase, an old-fashioned candlestick instrument, the receiver standing on end.

" Hallo, Josh ? "

" Everything all right, Mr. Mannering ? "

" I think so. I'm edgy, but——"

" I don't think you need worry about Mrs. Webber," Josh said earnestly. " I've just talked to her. If she *does* think it's too hot for her, she'll give you plenty of notice, Mr. Mannering. You just needn't worry."

" Thanks, Josh."

" It's all right about the folder," Josh said, and the worst of Mannering's glumness faded. " Mrs. Mannering hid it as soon as she came back from Maberley Square. Old B looked round but didn't find it, we've both memorised the names and addresses, and it's burnt."

" Wonderful ! " Mannering felt not only brighter, but almost exhilarated. " What about Farley ? "

" That's done, too."

" Has he agreed to act for me ? "

" Yes," said Larraby, and there was no longer any doubt, Mannering was exhilarated; it was always like this, too; blow hot, blow cold. " So it's all right as far as it goes, but I don't like Bristow's attitude at all. The flat's watched, the shop's watched, Carruthers said there was a Yard man in his street this morning. I slipped out to a kiosk from the shop, Bristow's coming to see me—he's found out I left home during the night. Don't let *that* worry you, but the build-up's pretty bad, Mr. Mannering. We've had the Press round of course, and Mr. Chittering——"

Mannering said sharply : " Yes ? " Chittering of the *Record* was both a friend and a reliable source of information.

" Mr. Chittering says that the Press has been asked to go all out," Larraby told him quietly. " The evening newspapers and tomorrow morning's, provincial as well as the London, will have your photograph. They're looking ! for your car, too—it wasn't in Maberley Square, remember."

" All right, Josh," Mannering said slowly. " Thank Chittering, be careful, don't take any chances when you ring up here. Tell Mrs. Mannering I've at least one other contact ready to help "—he did not mention old Sol— " and that it still won't last for long."

" It can't at this pressure," Larraby said. " Mr. Mannering, are you sure it wouldn't be wiser to give up ? They *can't* prove——"

" I can't move if I'm in a remand cell," Mannering said. " We'll do it this way, Josh."

" Bristow means to get you," Larraby was emphatic.

" He just won't leave a loophole. And Mr. Mannering, don't go near Judy Darrow. She's been transferred to a nursing home, the name of it will be in the newspapers this evening. Bristow probably thinks you'll go and see

her, it's the kind of thing he'd expect you to do. Be *very*
careful."

" You get Mr. Korra for me," Mannering said.

" I haven't a clue, yet," Larraby wasn't hopeful; or
cheerful. " Don't take any wild risks, will you ? "

" We'll get through," Mannering said.

CHAPTER IX

UNEASY DAY

IF there were a good thing during the day, it was the attitude
of Mrs. Webber. She didn't come up often, said little
when she did, proved that she was more than just a plain
cook, massaged Mannering's neck and shoulder with an
evil-smelling but soothing liniment, and brought him
several newspapers. The evening paper, which arrived
about four o'clock together with a piece of rich fruit cake,
gave the address of the nursing home to which Judy Darrow
had been taken. Larraby had been right about that ;
knowing that Mannering was desperate, Bristow would
expect him to strike in the least likely place.

And he had to see the girl.

He had to get to see Farley first.

It would not be dark until after eight o'clock, summer-
time had started the previous week-end ; and it wouldn't
be safe to move out until after dark. He must go to
Guildford. With nothing to do, little to work on, Mannering found himself studying the make-up on his face,
adding touches which really made no difference, wondering
whether he would be wise to go all out and disguise himself
completely. He might need to do that later ; he needed
some tricks up his sleeve.

The hours dragged. He massaged his neck and shoulder
again, both were much better and eating and talking were
less of a trial.

Soon after seven, Mrs. Webber brought up his ' supper '
—a generous portion of cod, fried golden brown, a heap
of chips, a fruit salad and Camembert cheese.

" The others don't care for it, too strong for them,
but I like a taste, myself," she said. " Thought you
would, too."

" You couldn't be more right. Are the others going
out again ? "

" Trust them ! Timmy's got to be off in half an hour,
always bolting his food, Timmy is. Jake'll be off at eight
on the dot, to see his girl-friend. Going out ? "

" As soon as it's dark."

" No one would ever recognise you, not without a close
look," said Mrs. Webber reassuringly. " You needn't
worry about that. Papers are going all out, aren't they ?—
not giving you much chance. If they catch you and they
find you've been here, Mr. Mannering, you won't let me
down, will you ? Won't mention Josh, either—*I'll* say
I didn't recognise you, and you paid in advance." Her
eyes twinkled. " Which you haven't ! "

" I won't let you down. And how much——"

" Forget it. Josh'll see that's squared up, I'm not
pushed for a quid or two. Josh said he would send you
some money, anyway. I'll just shout when the others
have gone, then you can come down."

" You're even better than Josh said you were. What
have you told them ? "

" That I've a gentleman in for a few days and not to
go messing around with his car," he said. " Timmy's
a fiend about engines, kill himself with his motor-bike
one of these days, he will."

Mannering said : " So he's got a motor-bike. Does he
go to work on it ? "

" No, only uses it evenings and week-ends. I'll call you,
don't forget, don't come down unless I have." She went
off, taking the tray with her, and Mannering surprised
himself by enjoying every mouthful ; Mrs. Webber was
good for his morale. He lingered over biscuits and the
Camembert, it was nearly eight o'clock when he had

finished ; and at a quarter past, she shouted upstairs.

" Ready whenever you like ! "

Clouds were blowing up, it wasn't dark but daylight was failing. Mannering made himself wait for another ten minutes, then went downstairs. Mrs. Webber was in the kitchen, washing up, big red arms bare to the elbows, blue smock gone and a white apron looking ridiculous over her plentiful bosom and barrel of a stomach.

" You off ? "

" Yes. Spare a key."

" Oh, I forgot. It'll be under the loose brick in the edging round the wallflowers. If you really want one your-self I can get one made, but——"

" No, provided you don't forget to put it out."

" I've told the others to leave it, whoever gets in last," she said. " Said you might be out late, you're going to see night life in London." She grinned. " Take care of yourself ! "

When he had arrived, he had turned the Buick so that he could drive straight out. The tank was full, but the car had been standing for several weeks, he ought to have the tyres and battery checked. He would do that later. He drove along the wide path and into Meybrick Road. Two or three people were walking along, a man glanced at the big Buick. Was it too noticeable ? He turned into a wider street, then into the Marylebone Road, where traffic was more plentiful, and a policeman strolled towards him. Most cars had their lights on. Mannering switched on his, watching the policeman out of the corner of his eye. He must get over this edginess ; there was no reason in the world why any policeman should take notice of the Buick, and without a close study no one would recognise him from photographs.

The edginess remained ; every policeman Mannering passed seemed to look towards him. At a junction one held him up for an old couple to cross the road. He should have waited until it was quite dark, his hands were tight on the wheel.

The policeman waved him on.

Mannering took the familiar road, towards Victoria, then Chelsea, Putney and on to the Kingston Road. Not until he was on the wide bypass could he put on any speed. It was quite dark, garages were brightly lit but there were few other lights except from cars.

Mannering judged that he would be at Guildford by about nine-thirty. It was surely safe to see Farley ; who could be more reliable than the solicitor acting for him ? It was safe—but there was a risk, there was always a risk. Farley wasn't the only one who lived near Guildford ; Lady Jane Creswell did. Mannering had often passed the gates of the Manor House in the old days. This area had been a happy hunting ground for the Baron —and probably more police in the Surrey country town knew him than anywhere else outside of London.

Was his disguise too thin ?

He drove through Cobham, passing only an occasional car. Traffic became thicker as he neared Guildford. He did not know where Lynton Avenue was ; residents on one side of the town might not know it, if it were on another. He drove along stone walls outside detached houses, and saw a taxi drawn up outside a house, sidelights on. He pulled up, got out and approached the driver.

" Lynton Avenue, sure—it's off the Leatherhead Road. You're not far away." The man gave instructions carefully, going into great detail. A man, out of sight, approached slowly ; Mannering associated slow and deliberate footsteps with policemen on the beat. He glanced towards the corner, as the cabby started to go over his directions again.

" Don't forget that first turn, *half* right. Not sharp right, see." He drew invisible pictures in the air with his forefinger. " Then it's easy. Second left . . ."

A policeman appeared at the corner and turned towards them. There was no bright light near, no need for urgent fears, but they came ; Mannering had to grit his teeth as he listened.

" . . . and then you're okay, on the main road, you can't miss it."

The policeman was nearly abreast of them.

" Thanks very much," Mannering said. " I've got that."

" Don't forget that *half*-right."

" I won't." To get back to the Buick, he had to face the policeman. The man was staring at the Buick, almost as if he were looking for that car in particular. Mannering thanked the cabby again. "Good night. Good evening, constable."

" Evening, sir." The policeman nodded sombrely and walked past. " Hallo, Ted."

" Why, hallo, Harry ! " The cabby wasn't tired of talking yet.

Mannering took the wheel, sat back and wiped the sweat off his forehead. He had to turn his wheels sharply to get past the taxi ; both driver and policeman saluted him. He took the first turning he'd been told of before he relaxed ; and a mood of exhilaration surged over him. Hadn't that kind of thing happened often enough in the past ? Only ill-luck would send a policeman who would recognise him ; his make-up wasn't *that* bad.

He followed the directions carefully, including the half-right, and after ten minutes he saw Lynton Avenue in the glow of his headlamps. He turned down it. The avenue was wide, the houses more modern than in the town itself. He could see white walls, white painted gates, lights at many of the porches and most of the windows ; several cars were standing by the kerb.

He drove the length of Lynton Avenue, a hundred yards or so, but didn't see the name of Farley's house— The Lawn. Several of the gates had nothing on them, or he could have missed the name. He turned in the road, went back, and found the house half-way along the road. No car stood outside it, there were lights at two downstairs windows, none upstairs. He pulled up out-side and sat for a few seconds in the car, lighting a cigarette automatically.

A man walked briskly from the end of the road and passed the car. Mannering got out, and the man looked

back. The drive gates of The Lawn were closed; there
was no light at the garage but he could just see it, almost
on a level with the front of the house. The drive was of
gravel and his footsteps were clear—if not so clear as
when he had walked along the pavement at Maberley
Square.

A path, showing faintly, led off the drive towards the
front door. Mannering took it, and stared at the windows.
The curtains of one lighted room were drawn, and he saw
a maid standing with her back to the window. The
other curtains were drawn. He reached the front door
and pressed the bell—and snatched his finger away as if
he had been burnt.

Could he trust Farley ?

He had spent all the afternoon thinking, and omitted
one obvious line of thought—one question which mattered.
Why had Farley asked him to buy the jewels ? Could
Farley have known the kind of trouble likely to result ?
Was Farley involved in the frame-up ?

Mannering could turn and run ; or he could try to
find out more. He stood on the porch, heard footsteps
and the handle turning. The light was behind the maid,
who said :

" Good evening, sir." She was older, much older,
than the trim girl at Maberley Square. The light wasn't
bright but it fell full on Mannering's face.

" Good evening. Is Mr. Farley in ? "

" Well, he's *in*, but have you an appointment ? "

" Just ask him if he can spare me ten minutes," Mannering said. " My name is Johnson." Any name would
do. " Tell him that he heard from my wife this morning."

" Will you come in, sir ? "

Mannering went in and the door closed behind him
and snapped shut. The maid gave a vague smile and
straightened her cap as she approached the door on the
right, the room where the curtains had been drawn.
She went in, interrupting a man's voice—not Farley's
or one which Mannering recognised—a smooth voice
with an overlay of culture which seemed just a veneer.

" Yes, Maude ? "

" There's a Mr. Johnson, sir, he——" the maid went in and closed the door. She seemed to be in the room a long time ; plenty of time for Farley to have identified a ' Johnson ' whose wife had talked to him that morning ; time enough for Farley to have called the police. Damn himself for a fool, why should he take it for granted that Farley——

The door opened.

" Will you come this way, sir, Mr. Farley won't be a moment." The maid turned towards the passage along-side the stairs, opened a door at the end of it, switched on a light to allow Mannering to pass. He went in, feeling as if this were a trap and there was no way out. Nerves were the trouble—he hadn't got them steady enough yet, of course he could trust Farley.

The room was different from anything he'd expected ; a bright morning-room, of yellows and pale greens, obviously more a woman's room than a man's. Mannering had a strong feeling that it was a young woman's ; it was very different, but somehow reminded him of the corner in Judy Darrow's room. He didn't sit down, but stubbed out his cigarette and lit another, looked at himself in a diamond-shaped mirror over the fireplace, tried again to convince himself that the disguise would serve—and heard Farley approach.

He swung round.

Farley, in a dinner jacket of old-fashioned cut, seemed to smile worriedly, as he came in and closed the door. His complete self-assurance had gone. He peered into Mannering's face—was he shortsighted ? It was an appreciable time before he said :

" So it is you—I didn't recognise you." He stood in front of Mannering, a taller man than he had seemed when sitting in his office. He still looked worried. " Man-nering, I can't tell you how sorry I am about the results of our agreement, but you shouldn't have come here. I'll gladly act for you, do anything I can to help, but you should have known better than to come here."

Mannering said slowly : " I won't stay long."

" I must ask you not to.   Unless——" Farley hesitated, seemed to relax, waved to a chair.   " But sit down."

" No, thanks."

" As you like."   Farley smiled ; it wasn't much of a smile, the kind of polite effort which he might sometimes make to a client for whom he had little time.   " As I'm acting for you, Mannering, you'll understand if I advise you to do what I think best.   You can guess what that is."

Mannering didn't guess aloud.   Farley looked embarassed and faintly disapproving, as if disappointed that Mannering did not help him out of an awkward situation.

" I'm sure you can guess.   You ought to give yourself up—running away can't help.   It's such a clear indication of your guilt that——" he paused, as if startled by something in Mannering's manner, backed a pace, and added : " I wish to God I'd never approached you.   I shall always feel responsible.   Why in heaven's name did you kill him ? "

CHAPTER X

DOUBTING FARLEY

MANNERING turned abruptly, pulled up a chair and sat down.   Farley watched him—and then became uneasy because of the way Mannering looked at him.   He took a chair himself, a small armchair which seemed too small for him.   He smoothed down his silvery hair with the palm of his hand.   The Farley of this bright room had none of the poise and assurance of the Farley of the London office.

Mannering said : " I didn't kill Blane, you idiot." He tried to speak lightly, to keep anger out of his voice. " That was done before I got there."

"Oh." Farley didn't try to argue, just didn't believe. Had the police got on to him, had they told him of the girl's statement? What else could make him feel so sure? "That's somewhat different, but——"

"I know, proving it will be quite a job," Mannering said. "I'll see to that. Are you representing Jacob Korra?"

Farley said: "Later, if it's necessary, I will name my client." He was still adamant, and would remain so.

"Who else wants those jewels?" Mannering demanded.

Farley said slowly: "I can understand your feeling, sympathise with your desire to try to find the—ah—murderer, but I still advise you to give yourself up. I should of course then make a full statement to the police; the fact that you knew of these jewels only yesterday would be helpful. While you remain at large, any statement I make will do more harm than good. You needn't commit yourself to any statement. You can talk freely to me first, then let me call the police, and I will watch your interests very closely. I already feel much responsibility, I'll——"

"Forget it, Farley, just tell me who else wants those jewels."

Farley said: "I know of no one."

"Except your client."

"That's right."

"I've told you, that is confidential."

"There are times to break confidences."

"I have to be judge of that," Farley said. He closed his lips, making his mouth look very thin. "Mannering, the obvious thing for you to do is——"

"To find out who killed Blane. As the jewels were stolen, it was probably someone after the jewels." That didn't follow; Farley could tear the reasoning to bits, but Mannering didn't give him a chance yet. "I only know of one man who wants them—your client."

"Yes," said Farley slowly, "you would think like that." He hesitated, then his voice grew firmer. "Mannering, I've had a great deal to do with people labouring under strong emotions, such as you are now. I know

how the mind works, and there are few stronger-willed
people than you. But it's easy to get the wrong idea,
to jump to conclusions which are quite false. My client
wants the jewels, but in no circumstances would he kill
for them. Obviously someone else wants them, if that
is why Blane was killed. There is an example of jumping
to conclusions. Blane may have been killed for simple
gain. The fact that the stolen jewels were those which
I asked you to buy may be incidental. I am talking from
the assumption that it wasn't you, of course."

" Hard to make the assumption, isn't it ? "

" Have you read all the evening papers, Mannering ? "

" Yes."

" Then you will have read that the girl Darrow made
a statement to the police. I know what that statement
was, and how damaging it is to you."

" I know, too, and I still didn't kill Blane or attack
her," said Mannering. His voice was mild ; more mild
than Farley deserved, but angering or frightening the
man wouldn't help. " I prefer to think that Blane was
killed for the jewels, and I'm anxious to see everyone
who wants them—such as your client."

" To suspect him is unthinkable."

" I could tell you other things that are unthinkable,"
Mannering said heavily. " Have you seen the police
yet ? "

" About this case ? No. I feel reluctant to, until
you are prepared to be interviewed."

" You'll be questioned, if they identify the jewels, won't
you ? "

" I think it unlikely," Farley said promptly. " Whether
I ought to volunteer a statement about it is a moot point,
of course, but acting for you, I have to protect your interests
as I think best." He stood up and spread out his hands,
warmth came into his voice and a kind of spurious friendliness. " Why don't you be a sensible chap, Mannering,
and see the police ? That would be much happier all
round—for yourself, your wife and——"

" Daniel Farley," Mannering said sardonically, " the

answer is still no. Talk to Jacob Korra, Farley, try suspecting that he's trying two ways to get the jewels. You might get some surprises." He stood up ; he didn't get any reaction from that ' Jacob Korra '. " Do you know Judy Darrow ? "

" No."

" As my lawyer, you might try finding out whether she is a reputable witness," Mannering said. " And also believing that I didn't kill Blane. Does anyone else know who might have the other jewels—the emeralds and the diamonds ? "

" Not to my knowledge."

" Isn't it time you told me more about them, even if you won't name your client ? " It wasn't easy to speak quietly ; it would have been easier to take hold of the solicitor and try to shake the information out of him— easier, and fatal to any hope of leaving Farley in any doubt about the murderer. " Who's Jacob Korra ? "

" That is the name of the original owner of all three sets of jewels. I've given you all the help I can, Mannering, but in the circumstances I don't expect you to try to find the other jewels—er, I mean, any of them," he added quickly.

Mannering found himself grinning.

" And you hope I don't, in case the other owners get strangled ! Don't worry too much—I've plenty to do saving my own neck."

" Let me try to persuade you again to look at this calmly and sensibly, Mannering, and——"

Mannering said : " I see it the way it is. You can do one of two things. Tell the police I've been here and why, or just keep quiet. If you've a conscience, you'll keep quiet. You're still acting for me, which shows what a forgiving nature I have."

" Mannering——"

" I have to be on my way," Mannering said. " I'm meeting my wife soon, I'd hoped to have cheerful news for her." He nodded and went towards the door. He wasn't satisfied with the way he had handled Farley, felt that he had got off on the wrong foot from the start and couldn't get on to the right one. " She'll tell you if there's anything I want you to do."

Farley said : " You're making a grave mistake, Mannering."

" Saying ' yes ' to you in the first place ? " asked Mannering.

He pushed past Farley and opened the door quickly ; no one was in the passage, although he had half expected to see someone. Farley followed but didn't call him back. Mannering reached the front door first, opened it, said ' Good night' over his shoulder, and went out." Farley echoed his ' good night ' faintly, and stood in the doorway. Mannering strode along the path, then to the drive. Farley couldn't see his car, except the top which showed just above the hedge—so whatever he told the police he couldn't describe the car. He probably thought that Mannering was really going to see Lorna, too. When Mannering reached the gate, the front door was closed, The Lawn looked exactly as it had when he had arrived. He didn't linger ; in two minutes he had turned out of Lynton Avenue and gone right, away from Guildford. The road was narrow and in parts winding ; it was some time before he found a stretch wide enough to pull into the side and stop. He drove on to a grass verge and switched off the engine.

What else could he have expected from Farley ?

He didn't waste time trying to answer that ; he had to decide on the next course, and now there was no certainty that Farley would withhold the story from the police. He had a feeling that Farley was nervous, and not only because of him. Farley might be wondering whether his other client was as innocent as he'd claimed.

That client wanted the Korra jewels badly. Someone else might be as anxious. Anyone who had part of the collection might long for the others—and that led his thoughts to Lady Jane Creswell and Aristotle Wynne ; they'd never been far away. Either might be able to tell him something about Korra, or about anyone else who had been anxious to get the jewels.

Blane had known that Korra was anxious, there might be others.

Mannering knew too little about the people in the case, nothing about Lady Jane Creswell, except that she lived only a few miles away. She might be old or young, she was probably wealthy—if he had not been on the run, he would have seen her after seeing Blane. He could still see her—the only question in his mind was whether to try to find out if she had any of the jewels; especially if she had the rubies.

He still needed to know more about Lady Jane and what she could tell him; she might know this Korra. He'd go to the Manor House. He'd pulled up to let himself think this over but had known what he would do almost before he'd stopped.

The decision carried its own peculiar sense of elation.

He had everything he needed; a set of cracksman's tools in the boot of the Buick would be the envy of a lot of swell mobsmen. It was either making the attempt or giving up, he couldn't just lie low. He started the car engine, glancing at his wristwatch; it was after ten o'clock. By twelve, most country households had retired for the night, the Manor was probably no exception. All he had to do now was drive to the nearest village— Melbury. That was on the Horsham side of Guildford, he had driven through it often on the way to the South Coast.

The chief danger was from Farley; but Farley would probably decide to sleep on what he knew before taking any decision. He damned Farley as he turned the car and made for Guildford, bypassed the town and reached the Horsham Road on the far side of it. The drive to Melbury would take little more than half an hour, he would have some waiting to do. He could use part of the time calling Lorna, but an out-of-London call could be traced, he mustn't risk it.

Would it be safe to take a room in a hotel in the village ? Or nearby ? No identification would be called for, no one would look up and think ' Mannering ' but it might set minds thinking ; he had better stick to the car. He wished it were earlier ; the pubs were closed, and Farley, damn the man, hadn't even offered him a drink.

Just before eleven, he was in Melbury ; by ten minutes past, he was at the drive gates leading to the Manor.

* * *

Mannering parked the car in a field behind a haystack, and shut the five-barred gate of the field behind him. A fitful moon, new two days earlier, shone through gaps in heavy clouds. If it rained, it would be heavier rain than the night before. The ground was soft underfoot as he walked from the field to a stile which led to the grounds of the Manor. He had driven round the house, along two lanes, with light enough from the moon to see the copses, dark against the sky, the sweeping parkland dotted with trees in front of the house itself ; and the house. From a distance it was a dark pile, broad and heavy where it stood on the top of a slope. Two lights shone at windows which he judged were upstairs ; he couldn't be sure. He climbed the stile and walked towards the nearer copse. It was half past eleven.

He waited, moving quietly about the grass beneath the trees, watchful and alert. He wanted the lights at the windows to go out ; and he wanted to make sure that no one in the village or on the narrow road leading to it had noticed his headlights and come to investigate ; village policemen had a notorious curiosity and a high sense of duty.

It was warm. His shoulder was only slightly stiff ; his neck troubled him a little when he turned his head sharply but if he were cautious, neither would interfere with his actions.

He had the tools in a canvas holder, worn round his waist like a belt ; everything needed to break into the average country house and force the average country safe was at his hand. He didn't think about the mechanical task of getting into the Manor, just took that for granted ; the Baron could have taught most locksmiths tricks they didn't know.

The quietness of the countryside soothed him.

The first light at the Manor went out at ten minutes to twelve; the second, at twelve o'clock. He heard no sound suggesting that anyone was approaching, saw no wavering light of a cyclist coming uphill. He left the cover of the copse, knowing he could not be seen. The moon was low, but the clouds were breaking up and it shone most of the time, just a pale glow. He was soon within the shadow of the Manor, a stone-built house with mullioned windows, not typical of Surrey. He could make out two open windows on the first floor; one on the third and top floor. He avoided the front door but saw the round pillars supporting the porch, the heavy ledges at windows.

A gravel path ran round the house, changing direction here and there because of flower beds; and everywhere damp turf deadened his footsteps; the omens were good. A side door faced east, the windows on that side overlooked the village but he could not see even the tall spire of the church. A rose garden, the beds cut out of the lawn, ran downhill on this side, and he made out the shape of the protecting nets of a tennis court.

At the back were outbuildings—stables and garages. The moon glistened on the glass of two long greenhouses; beyond them was a walled garden. In spite of the darkness, Mannering had an impression of well-kept grounds, everything would be in its rightful place. The back of the house had several rooms, probably wash and store houses, all one storey—made for climbing. The approach to the back door was roofed-in and pitch dark. All the doors were likely to be locked and bolted, a first-floor window was his best bet—an open one would save a lot of trouble.

He had heard no sound, no dog barked, no light was visible. He stood back, peering above the tiled roof of an outhouse, looking at the windows; at the back they were of the sash cord type, easy to open with the right tool. He saw one immediately above a roof-ledge where he could stand securely and which he could reach easily.

He pulled on a pair of rubber gloves, which fitted skin-tight
—almost as free as his natural skin; then he started up.

CHAPTER XI

LADY JANE

MANNERING walked softly along a carpeted landing towards
the stairs, only his slim pencil torch showing the way.
The house had been silent when he had forced the window
and climbed into a bathroom; it was silent now. He
had been along every passage, up three flights of stairs,
and had a mind-picture of the house. He had unbolted
and unlocked the outside doors, could make a quick getaway
if an alarm were raised.

Mannering reached the spacious hall, where white
paint and pale walls seemed to make the light brighter;
it reflected from the glass in front of pictures, from polished
furniture. The carpet sank beneath his feet, thick pile
with a thick felt; everything had confirmed what he had
thought in the grounds—this house was well maintained,
belonged to wealthy people.

He went into the room on the left of the stairs, the right
of the front door; the curtains were drawn, he had seen
that on his first visit. He closed the door and switched
on a light; in fact several lights shone, over pictures
round the walls of a small room, exquisitely furnished
in Louis Quinze style. The soft glow was a relief after
the strain of walking through dark passages with only
a thin beam to show him the way.

He pulled a chair closer to the door, and sat down.

He had heard tiny sounds; the night noises of a house,
which might alarm the nervous and puzzle the stranger.
None of them had mattered. He would hear if anyone
came down the stairs or approached the house, but he
thought of that with only half his mind, it was almost

instinctive. He pictured the two main floors—this and the one abóve. Above that again were the servants' quarters and a big games' room; he was likely to find nothing that would help there.

Above him was a dressing-room; next to that over the drawing-room, a large bedroom where a woman had lain sleeping. He had not gone far enough in to look at her closely. In a smaller room, across the landing, another elderly woman lay asleep. No one else was on that floor. Above them were three servants; man and wife together in a double bed, and a girl in an adjoining room. He had locked the servants in their rooms and left the keys in the doors.

The main bedroom might have a safe. On the same floor, opposite it, was a study-cum-library, reminding him of Blane's room; the safe might be there. On this floor, the most likely place was in the dining-room. Mannering had found no entrance to a cellar or to strong-rooms; that didn't mean there was none—it might be cleverly concealed.

He satisfied himself that he knew the lay-out of the house, that wherever he was he would know which way to turn to get out. He had seldom been in a house by night with less feeling of danger, and the fact teased him; it could be a false sense of security.

He let the thought fade, stood up, put out the light and went into the dining-room, across the hall. The curtains were drawn in there, too, but he crossed to them, pulled two closer so that they overlapped before he switched on a light. This room was early Georgian; everything was right, the gleaming mahogany furniture, the Persian carpet, the oil paintings, all of them good. He stood by the door. If a safe were here, the sideboard, a huge piece of carved mahogany which stretched almost the length of the wall behind the door, was the probable place of concealment. Silver-plate—or perhaps real silver —was mirrored on the shining surface. There were three doors.

He knelt down and tried the first; it was open. The

middle one was locked ; so was the third. He unbuttoned
his coat and took a pick-lock from the waistband, slipped
it into the key-hole, twisted, and had the lock back in
thirty seconds. The door opened to show drawers one
upon the other—probably of cutlery. Each drawer was
locked.

Now that he had started, he took infinite pains ; minutes
saved now might cost him an hour later on, or make him
come back to a job he should have done. There were
five drawers ; each was neatly filled with silver cutlery,
with a crest on the handles. He closed and locked them
one after the other, then re-locked the door. He stood
up, to ease his legs, went to the hall door and listened
intently, was satisfied, and came back this time to the
middle cupboard. It opened on to an ordinary steel
safe which fitted comfortably inside. The safe bore
the maker's name—it was an early Landon—and had two
keyholes, each marked round the edges. This should
be simple to open.

It was proving easy. Too easy ? Burglary *was* easy,
unless a house or a safe were equipped with the most
modern methods of protection. This house didn't seem
to be ; there were no burglar alarms, no wires, just the
old-fashioned safe. He didn't start work on it at once
but studied it, seeing in his mind's eye the mechanism
of the lock, mentally choosing the tools to start with.
The two locks placed its period—it was thirty or forty
years old. The upper lock had to be turned first, the
second could not be opened until the first was free. There
were variations in the locking mechanism ; a safe like
this had once nearly blinded him—gas had spurted out
as he had forced the second lock. There was nothing to
indicate unusual precautions here, but he was slow,
deliberate, thoughtful. If it opened easily, it would be
almost too good to be true.

The first lock turned under the pressure of a tool made
for its type. There was no trouble.

He moved to one side before starting on the other
lock, prepared for a spurt of gas or flame but not expecting

it. The twisting and turning took longer, but the lock turned at last. He heard the click.

He paused, wiped his forehead with the back of his hand, then turned the handle slowly, still keeping out of direct line with the door ; only his hand would suffer and the rubber glove would save it. The handle turned easily, and when he pulled the door moved as if it were well-oiled. No tricks, no catch. Satisfied, he moved in front of it.

There were jewel-cases on one shelf ; documents and a cash-box on the other ; nothing else. He took out the documents, most of them tied in red tape, like some in Farley's office. Deeds of various properties, deeds of agreement between Lady Jane Creswell and people he didn't know—and then a small document on stiff paper, and the words :

Agreement
Between
Lady Jane Creswell
and
Jacob Korra Melano Esquire
June 1st 1939

Korra wasn't the full name, then; Larraby wasn't likely to find that out easily.

Mannering studied the copper-plate handwriting for a few moments, feeling the thrill of some success, resisted the temptation to read it at once, put it to one side and finished looking through the others. Nothing interested him until he reached the last, a foolscap envelope, yellowy-brown in colour—an American make, not sealed but fastened with a metal clasp. He undid this and took out the papers.

They were three sheets identical with those that Farley had given him ; photographs of the Korra emeralds, with the dimensions and colours ; everything was exactly the same as on one of the sheets which Lorna had burnt. Mannering began to smile as he laid these on the Korra Melano agreement. There was nothing else in the envelope. He eased his legs again, stood by the door, beginning to feel that it was going so smoothly that he would get a shock before he finished ; he had never had a trouble-free night's work without feeling that. It meant nothing, served only to keep him wary.

He went back and looked at the jewel-cases, then took them out. He felt his pulse beating faster. The cases weren't locked, but that meant nothing, too many people thought that a locked safe was all the security needed. He opened the first, and felt the first disappointment ; two diamond rings and a diamond brooch were valuable but not remarkable, nothing like the Korra jewels. He opened three more cases ; all contained diamond jewellery, none was what he wanted to find.

He put everything back except the one document, crossed the room again, put out the light and opened the door. Only the dark silence greeted him, no sound except the odd creaks and whimpers as if ghosts were walking ; nothing to scare him. He closed the door, put on the light, went to a heavy, carved mahogany chair and sat down at the table, opening the document.

It was short—just three paragraphs. It was an agreement between Jacob Korra Melano and Lady Jane Creswell who, for a consideration of one thousand pounds a year, agreed to serve on the boards of three companies, all named by Korra—but the companies weren't listed. The agreement had been for seven years, so had lapsed years ago. The promise of Mannering's discovery fell away, all it did was to confirm an association between Korra and the woman who lived here—and who was probably sleeping in the big room upstairs.

Nothing Mannering had found really helped him.

He put the document back in the safe, decided not to read through the others but read the name of the solicitors ; Daniel Farley wasn't mentioned, this was a reputable firm in Lincoln's Inn. Mannering closed the door and locked the safe ; no one was ever likely to know that it had been forced, for he made a clean job of it, locking both locks as easily as he had opened them.

Still wary, he went to the door, put out the light, looked
into darkness, and stepped into the hall. Then he
took out the pencil torch. The silence began to wear
on his nerves—that was partly reaction from disappointment as well as from the completion of the first task. The
certain thing was that Lady Jane Creswell knew Korra,
could tell him something about Korra and perhaps where
to find the man.

He went upstairs, walked along the three passages,
made sure no light was on and nothing stirred, then went
to the main bedroom over the drawing-room. Only
his torchlight showed him the bed and the sleeping woman,
the wardrobe, the smaller furniture. He went to the
room where the old woman slept, locked her door, and
came back and went close to the younger woman for the
first time.

Her face was turned towards the window. Her hair
was dark, almost black—the hair of a young woman, or
dyed ? He went to the side of the bed, back to the window
and the dressing-table, and shone the torch so that he
could see the woman's face.

He felt the shock as if it were physical, for he looked
into a face so like Judy Darrow's that in the first startled
moment, he thought it was the girl. The moment passed
as swiftly as it came ; this woman was older—in the late
thirties, probably. Her face showed no traces of excessive
make up. Her skin was rather greasy, as if she had rubbed
cream well in before retiring. Her lashes and eyebrows
were dark and clearly marked.

She stirred and turned her head.

The likeness to the girl remained but Mannering saw
one difference ; this woman was more truly beautiful.
She stirred again, drew an arm from the bedclothes, bare
to the shoulder—the nightdress was pale yellow. He
stretched out a hand and switched on the light at the bedside table ; it fell fully on to her face, and this time she
not only stirred ; her eyelids fluttered. Mannering stood
back from the bed, and spoke softly, keeping all expression
out of his voice, killing menace.

" Wake up, Lady Jane. Don't worry, just wake up."

Her eyes fluttered open, and her features became stiff
with fright. The light dazzled her, but she could probably
make out the figure of a man. She didn't move her body,
just kept rigid, with her lips parted.

" Don't panic, I won't hurt you," Mannering said.

Her lips relaxed, she began to move herself higher on
her pillow, turning her head a little and avoiding the glare
from the light.

" Unless you shout or try to raise an alarm," Mannering
said.

Her lips moved.

" I—I won't." She sat up further, put a hand behind
her to push the pillow up. "Who—who are you?"
She was frightened, who wouldn't be? but her voice didn't
tremble. "What do you want?"

" Information," he said. " The truth."

" What—what about?"

" Jacob Korra Melano and his jewels."

Mannering could judge nothing from the woman's
expression, unless it were a hint of distaste at the name
Korra. She had the pillow where she wanted it, and sat
almost erect. The nightdress was high at the neck ; she
was full breasted but not heavy.

" I haven't seen Korra for years," she said, and drew
her hand away from the pillow.

She acted as she talked, quite calmly. She seemed as
if she were used to holding the gun, which was steady in
her hand and pointing at his chest.

CHAPTER XII

LADY WITH A GUN

THE woman's calmness startled Mannering as much as
the gun. She had pulled that out neatly, almost as if

she had practised the trick. She was two yards away from him; he couldn't swing his arm and knock it out of her hand. The gun covered his chest steadily, and she looked into his eyes. Hers were as calm as her manner.

"Move back," she said.

He obeyed, watching her, beginning to smile; the smile touched his eyes first, then spread to his lips.

"Further."

He touched the dressing-table with his left leg, and was within a yard of the window. He could move his left hand and pick up something to throw from the dressing-table, but he kept both hands in sight, and his smile became wider. That didn't affect her, yet. She clutched the bedclothes with her free hand and flung them back, careful not to let any of them touch the gun. She wore pyjamas, one leg was rucked up about the knee. She slid her legs out of the bed, keeping the gun remarkably steady.

Mannering laughed.

"You won't think this is funny much longer," she said softly.

"You're magnificent!"

She had pulled her backless slippers into position, but didn't slip her feet into them; frowned, as if she couldn't understand Mannering's amusement or the mockery in that last word. She stood up, slowly, and pushed her feet into the slippers.

"Can I get you your dressing-gown?" asked Mannering politely.

"Just keep still."

"I daren't move!"

"If you move, I'll shoot you," she said, as she crossed in front of him and backed towards the wall, more cautious and perhaps a shade less confident than she had been at the beginning. She put her left hand behind her, to grope for a bell-push which was by the side of the fire-place.

"A few inches to your right and further back," said

Mannering helpfully, " but I shouldn't send for help yet."

She backed again, and came up against a chair.

" You obviously don't need help," Mannering said, " and all I want is information. Why don't you sit down, Lady Jane ? "

That startled her. It would hardly be because he knew her name. Her hand fell to her side, as if she were wondering whether it would be such a good idea to send for help. She lowered herself gradually on to the chair. The gun hadn't wavered.

" If you'd gone into Lady Jane's room, the shock might have killed her," she said.

So she wasn't Lady Jane.

Mannering didn't question that, and was too intent on the gun to be annoyed by his wrong guess. The woman brushed a lock of her black hair from her forehead. She was beautiful—handsome might be the better word— and she had poise. The likeness to Judy Darrow was remarkable, it was easy to understand his first shock of surprise. Judy's mother ? The girl was in her early twenties, this woman might be in the early forties.

" People seldom die of shock," Mannering murmured.

" She is very old, she——" the woman stopped, as if annoyed to find herself wasting time in talking to him. " Keep where you are, I'm going to ring for help." She had to stand up again, to get at the bell-push, and as she put her left arm behind her she thrust herself forward, emphasising the magnificence of her figure. The yellow pyjamas fitted loosely at the waist, tightly at her breast.

She groped again for the bell-push, not daring to look away from Mannering.

" If you must ring, why not let me press the bell ? " asked Mannering obligingly. " I won't—— "

He cut the words off and glanced swiftly towards the door, catching his breath. The woman was fooled, and looked towards the door—and he leapt at her. She realised what was happening a fraction of a second too late; he caught her wrist and forced her arm upwards. The chair fell over with a crash. The gun went off, roaring in their ears, the bullets smashed into the ceiling and a shower of plaster and dust fell down. Close together, her right and his left arm stretching upwards, they struggled for mastery. She wasn't a weakling and the sudden strain brought pain back to his shoulder and his neck. He gripped her left arm with his right hand and forced it downwards. She still struggled but with constricted movements; he could feel her breath on his cheeks, see the fear in her eyes.

"Let the gun go," Mannering said harshly. "You'll get hurt if you don't. "Let it go."

She lowered her head and tried to butt his nose. He bent his head back in time, pain shot through the side of his neck. He twisted her right wrist, almost savagely, and she relaxed. He felt her muscles slackening. A sudden snatch, and he had the gun. He let her go, backing away swiftly. She stood close to the wall, gasping for breath; that was the only sound he heard, and it could drown the sound of anyone approaching. He reached the wardrobe; the room door was on his left, she was by the fireplace in front of him; he could watch both her and the door.

"Come away from the wall," he ordered.

She didn't move.

"Come away!" He couldn't make her, except by frightening her. The handle of the door didn't turn and her breathing wasn't so loud, but he still couldn't be sure that he would hear anyone approaching from outside. The last echoes of the shot had faded, even from his ears. A dusting of powder and a few chippings were on the carpet and on the woman's hair.

Mannering's look succeeded where his voice failed. She came away from the fireplace slowly—too far away to swing round and press the bell. Mannering let her come as far as the foot of the bed.

"That's far enough."

She stopped. Mannering edged sideways towards the

door until he reached it. Now he could hear only the
normal sound of the woman's breathing—nothing from
outside. It was a big house, the walls were thick, the old
woman might not have heard, and the servants might still
be asleep in their locked room.

Mannering relaxed, and pointed to the woman's dressing-
gown, which hung over the foot of the bed.

" Put that on, it's chilly." It was cold. She was beginning to shiver but that was probably as much from
nervous reaction as anything else. She obeyed; and her
movements as well as her face and figure reminded
him of Judy Darrow. She put her hands to her head
and brushed the hair back, a little gesture that drew
her hair straight back from her forehead, much the style
that the girl used. "Do you keep anything to drink up
here ? "

She hesitated. " No. No, we don't."

" We could both do with a drink. Let's go downstairs."
He grinned as he spoke.

She began to smile ; it was partly to cover nervousness,
partly because he seemed to mean her no harm.

" You believe in making yourself at home, don't you ? "
She didn't move except to massage her right wrist ; he'd
hurt that.

" Come over to the door," he ordered.

She obeyed, and he backed away, made her open the
door and peered on to the landing, satisfied himself that
no one was about, then told her to go downstairs. If
she chose, she could run for the passage and the staircase
leading to the servants' quarters ; she couldn't be sure
that he would shoot but she couldn't be sure that he
wouldn't. She did just what she was told, and by the
time they reached the hall, was much more composed.
She led the way into the small room where he had sat
to get the lay-out of the house clear in his mind. From a
small cabinet, pseudo Louis Quinze, she took bottles,
glasses and a syphon.

" What will you have ? " she asked, and then the ab-
surdity of it struck her, and she began to laugh, weakly ;

nervous reaction. She kept laughing for what seemed a long time. Mannering stood and smiled at her crookedly until she recovered.

"A whisky and soda sounds fine."

She poured whisky, said 'say when' and when the drink was ready, poured herself one; she splashed plenty of soda into her glass. Her hands shook a little.

"Put mine on that table," Mannering said, and pointed. "Then you can go back for yours."

That kept a safe distance between them. When she had put his drink down, he went across to it, slipped the gun into his pocket, waved to a chair and sat down himself. She was completely relaxed, now, was smiling most of the time, with a kind of reluctant admiration.

"I never expected to meet a burglar like you." She forced herself to talk down her nervousness.

"That's the sad part of our profession," Mannering said sorrowfully, "people only meet the worst of us. Do you work for Lady Jane?"

"Yes."

"Housekeeper, counsellor and friend, and the best bedroom, too."

"She likes the little room, it gets more sun and keeps warmer."

"How long have you been with her?"

"For too long—fifteen years. I can't leave her now, she's almost helpless."

There must be a reason why a woman with her looks and poise, her mind and her resource, should waste her life looking after an old woman. The reason didn't really matter, but Mannering was as curious about that as about anything else.

"Who are you?"

"Mrs.——" she hesitated, laughed uncertainly again, and went on: "Stella Darrow."

"Thank you, Mrs. Darrow. Now believe it or not, all I want is information about Jacob Korra Melano and— his jewels." He sipped as he finished, but watched her closely. The word 'jewels' made her start and took the smile away, she became more wary. " Lady Jane has the emeralds, hasn't she ? "

Stella Darrow said slowly : " Yes. How did you know ? "

" Forget it.   Had she got them here ? "

" No.   She sold them."

" When and to whom ? "

The woman hesitated. Mannering didn't take out his gun, but spoke very softly ; she could feel the menace.

" You're going to talk, if I have to get rough to make you."

" About five years ago—to a dealer." She was sure he meant what he said.

" Are you sure it was a dealer ? "

" Yes," she said. " I can't imagine why you're interested.   She sold them to a man she used to know, he's in Cornwall now.   Aristotle Wynne.   He paid her twenty-one thousand pounds for them.   They were worth more, but she needed the money and she *didn't* particularly want those emeralds."   The woman talked quite freely now, as if she knew there would be no danger provided she did that.

" Why not ? "   Mannering asked.

" She'd come to hate Jacob Korra and everything to do with him," said Stella Darrow. " It's no use asking me to explain that, you can't explain the way a woman's mind works when she's nearly eighty."

" You can never explain how a woman's mind works," Mannering said, and grinned—to cover his surprise that Lady Jane Creswell had been ' nearly eighty ' five years ago   " Why don't you call him Melano ? "

" He always used Korra," the woman said. " It was his trade name.   Don't ask me why he dropped the Melano."

" How well did Lady Jane know him ? "

" Very well, I think—they'd been acquaintances for years before I came here.   He handled most of her business for her."

" Honestly ? "

" I think so. Lady Jane knew Korra's wife better than she knew Korra himself. I don't think she ever liked Korra, but she hadn't much of a business head and he had a good one. You say you want to know about the Korra jewels." She hesitated; he wondered if she were preparing to tell him the truth or a lie. " He bought them for his wife, who was very beautiful—much younger than he. There were three exquisite sets—emeralds, to match her eyes, rubies to match her lips, diamonds because Korra always had to have the best of everything." Stella Darrow wasn't exactly laughing at Mannering, but looked as if she wondered whether he were really interested in such sentimental associations; she seemed to have lost her fear completely. "His wife looked best in the emeralds but looked superb in anything." Her expression changed, was almost sombre. " I didn't have much time for Jacob Korra but I felt sorry for him when she died."

So Korra's beautiful young wife had died and the jewels he had collected for her had been sold—the last thing a man would sell if he deeply mourned, unless he were forced to.

Mannering had assumed that Korra was a wealthy man.

" How long ago did she die ? " asked Mannering.

" Ten years," said Stella Darrow. " He went to pieces completely. A business partner cheated him, he lost nearly everything he possessed. He would have gone bankrupt but for his wife's jewels. He was here when he first decided to sell them." The woman's voice was quiet but somehow reflected the poignancy of the scene, the torment in the mind of the man who had been compelled to sell the precious things which had adorned the girl he had loved. " He wanted Lady Jane to buy them all but she couldn't afford to. He wanted to make sure that someone who knew his wife had them, but it just wasn't possible. Jane had always liked the emeralds. She paid thirty thousand pounds for them. I didn't know where the others went, only that Korra sold them—until

five years ago, when Aristotle Wynne came to see if Lady
Jane would sell the emeralds and said that he'd bought
the diamonds years ago. I was astonished, because——"

She broke off, staring at Mannering, who wasn't paying
attention, was getting up slowly. Another sound fell into
the quiet of the room—that of a car not far away.

Stella Darrow jumped up.

The car was coming nearer, along the drive.

CHAPTER XIII

NIGHT ARRIVAL

THE car was moving quickly, sounded so near that it
seemed likely to stop at any moment. Mannering dropped
his hand to his pocket but didn't draw the gun out. The
woman stood up, staring in bewilderment towards the
door.

" Who on earth can that be ? "

It could be the police—the police were a constant menace ;
never mind wondering what would bring them here in
the small hours.

" Turn round," Mannering said abruptly.

She looked at him, alarm flooded her eyes.

" You still won't get hurt if you do what you're told.
Make for the cloakroom under the staircase." He didn't
show the gun but thrust it against his pocket. She hesitated.
She could scream, or she could take a chance and run
out of the room, slamming the door on him, and he wouldn't
shoot. She didn't know that, it was his strong suit.
" Hurry ! "

She turned her back on him and went to the door. The
car stopped, wheels crunching on the gravel. Whoever
had arrived would have seen the light in the room.

A car door slammed.

Stella Darrow reached the cloakroom door.

" Inside," he said. " We'll finish the chat another day."
He grinned at her, opened the door, and took her elbow ;
she went in without a protest. He closed the door and
turned the key in the lock, didn't take the key out, but
opened the back door. He could hear footsteps from the
front, and a bell rang somewhere a long way off. One
would ring in the domestic quarters, another probably
upstairs. He slipped into the garden. This doorway
was towards the side of the house, the single storey outbuildings were on his right. He closed the door firmly,
then hurried on to the grass and towards the side of the
house and the drive.

The moon had set, but the stars were out ; it was a fine
clear night ; cold, invigorating. Keeping to the grass,
Mannering turned a corner of the house and saw the glow
of car headlights shining his way. He went closer to the
wall as he turned the corner.

The car was a small sports model, an M.G. The police
didn't travel about in M.G.'s, there had never been any
reason to think the police had come. Mannering couldn't
see anyone, but whoever it was would be on the porch.
One caller, or two ? He hadn't been near enough to
judge from the footsteps. He stepped on to a flower
bed and felt flowers bend and break, reached the wall
again beside a climbing rose, and heard a man say :

" He's a hell of a time ! "

A girl said : " He's right at the top of the house, David,
even if the bell woke him first time, he couldn't get down
yet."

The voice and the way the girl spoke identified her ;
Judy Darrow and a young man named David were on
the porch.

*　　*　　*

Mannering had come round here to find out if he knew
the callers, expecting to find strangers, prepared to race
towards the narrow lane, the five-barred gate and the
Buick. If he'd made for the Buick straight away he
wouldn't have known that the girl was here.

He stood quite still, heart pounding.

She had been transferred from a hospital to a nursing home, the Press accounts had suggested she would be there for some time. Had that been to fool him and lure him to try to see her ? Had she left with the approval of the police ? Whether she had or not, they would surely have followed her. Wherever Judy Darrow was, the police weren't likely to be far away—unless she had slipped them. Why should she do that ?

"It's damned cold," said the young man named David. "If he doesn't come soon, I'll smash a window. I—say, Judy ! "

"*Please* don't fuss, David, it's so late."

"But the lights were on in that room at the side. Remember ? "

"Yes, they were," said Judy Darrow, wonderingly. She didn't sound as if she ought to be in bed. "That's strange. Perhaps Lady Jane was restless."

"If someone's up, why haven't they answered ? " There were footsteps, a man appeared vaguely in the reflected light of the headlamps, stepped from the porch and looked at the windows, as if hoping one would be open. "No luck." He wasn't twenty yards away from Mannering who stood absolutely still. "Put your finger on the bell and keep it there, I'll have a look round."

"We mustn't break in, it will frighten them. Look and see if the light's on in Old Sam's room. It's on the top floor at the back."

"It had better be on." David walked quickly towards Mannering, who stood half concealed by the fronds of the climbing rose, didn't glance his way, walked past and disappeared round the corner. Judy Darrow, on her own was on the porch. He could get to her, silence her, carry her to the M.G., be a mile away before David heard the engine and came rushing. There was nothing in the world that Mannering wanted more than a long talk with Judy Darrow.

The police ?

From where he stood he could see any lights for miles

around; there was none. If the police had followed her, they were being canny about it, and they couldn't get far without lights. If she had slipped away from the nursing home secretly, fooling them, the police might have no idea where she had come. But David would raise an alarm, when he realized she was missing, the hunt would be up for the M.G.

No one would look for a Buick.

There would probably never be another chance of the heart-to-heart talk with Judy. What was he waiting for? Supposing the police had followed—he would be on the look-out, could let her go at the first threat. David would be near the back of the house by now, craning his neck to look at the top windows.

Mannering moved forward silently over the grass, reached the entrance to the porch and saw Judy standing, her back towards him, a finger on the bell-push; she couldn't have kept it on all the time. She heard nothing, seemed to suspect nothing. Mannering stepped on to the porch, his scarf between his hands. She was beginning to turn round, just a shadowy figure. He raised the scarf above her head, thrust forward, brought it tight against her mouth and nose and pulled.

She screamed; the sound was lost in the muffling scarf. He felt her body go rigid. She fell against him as he tied the scarf, doubled the knot, then swung her round by her shoulder and lifted her.

She struck out wildly, but couldn't help herself. It was only a step to the open M.G. Mannering lifted her over the side, dumped her in the seat, and said harshly:

" If you move, I'll slap you down."

David couldn't have reached the back of the house yet. Mannering opened the door and slid into the driving-seat and the girl struck at his hand as he groped for the ignition key which was still in position.

He pushed her hand away roughly.

" I don't *want* to hurt you." He twisted, and pulled the self-starter, the engine turned over. " Keep quiet and——"

She couldn't shout, but she stood up, striking at him again, then put a leg over the side. He pulled her back, his movements restricted in the small space, managed to get a grip on her wrists, held them together with one hand, took a small twist of cord from the tool-kit and tried to wind it round her wrists.

David would be on his way back now, might even have heard the ticking-over of the engine. The girl fought desperately but Mannering coiled the cord round her wrists and used both hands to tie it. That wouldn't last long but she was helpless for the moment. He put the car in gear, took off the brakes and nosed round the circular carriageway. There was no sound from behind him.

Judy kicked sideways, caught Mannering's ankle and made him wince; she was a fighter, if she hadn't lied about him he could have admired her. He kicked back, and she gasped and stopped trying. The car faced the drive now. He put it into neutral and coasted down—and there was still no sound from behind them. David was probably looking for an open window.

Mannering switched on the headlamps. Grass, the pale yellow drive, trees near the edges, all showed up—and, a long way off, the drive gates. A rabbit leapt across the drive and disappeared. Mannering put the car into gear again. The girl kept still. Mannering saw nothing in front of him or in the range of the headlamps. If the police were watching, they would be near the gates, car lights doused. He looked right and left, almost holding his breath, swung out of the drive and towards the narrow lane, the five-barred gate and the Buick.

The engine roared, hedges scraped against the side of the M.G. the girl kicked at him again but he took no notice. He saw the stile, the copse beyond and the gate showed up in the headlights. He slowed down, stopped smoothly, and before the girl knew what he was doing, jumped out and went round to her. Her eyes glistened in the starlight, and she had freed her wrists—she struck at him again.

" So you want to be hurt," Mannering said.

He didn't like it, but he struck her sharply beneath the chin—that ought to put her out. Her head went back, then lolled forward. She would have a bruise, that was all. He unlatched the gate and pushed it back and carried her to the Buick.

Two minutes well spent now and he would have less trouble later on. He pulled the loosened cord free, tied her wrists more tightly, cut off a length of cord and tied her ankles. He was breathing heavily and his shoulder was aching.

He lifted her into the Buick, sat her so that she looked as if she was asleep ; not that there would be many passers-by.

No one, nothing stirred.

Mannering drove out of the gateway, turned right towards the village, with only inches between the Buick and the M.G. That would soon be found ; and the police would be here within the hour, less if David acted quickly. The police would find the tyre marks of the Buick, their first real clue. Forget it, just concentrate on getting away.

Where to ? Where could he have the quiet chat with Judy ?

London and Mrs. Webber ? The Landlady would stand a lot but she probably wouldn't stand for that. He hadn't a place to hide—but he had a place to go to for more information about Korra. Cornwall wasn't so far away, it could be reached in a day from London, easily. He could be a hundred miles away from here before many people were about.

What was the best route ? Horsham, across country to Winchester, then Salisbury or a road south of it, on towards Honiton in Devon. The roads would be empty. The headlights fell on the hedgerows, then on the windows of the cottages in the villages, on to the church, then on to the open road. Soon they were on a main road with telegraph posts on either side, but there was no traffic— just welcome emptiness. He kept an eye on the driving mirror; no one was behind him, David was probably by the M.G., fuming, storming.

In twenty minutes, Mannering had covered fifteen miles, including the winding road from the five-barred gate through Melbury. Now the needle quivered between sixty and seventy, he slowed down only at curves and at signposts. The girl began to move, but she hadn't really come round. Ten more minutes and ten more miles passed before she sat upright, really awake. Mannering glanced at her. Her face was turned towards him, and he could see her eyes clearly.

" You asked for it," he said.

She spoke through the scarf but he couldn't understand the words. Without the scarf she would probably shout; if they passed a village and met a constable, she would try to attract his attention; better let her stay as she was. She could move her legs, he hadn't tied them tightly. If he loosened the cord at her wrists, she might try some funny stuff, and he couldn't risk that at speed.

He sensed that she was looking straight ahead of her.

They could go on like this during the darkness but when light came, he would have to take the scarf away.

What time was it ? He couldn't see his wristwatch clearly. About one, when he had woken Stella Darrow— say half past two. It couldn't be later than half past two, could it ? That would give him two and a half hours or more, or a hundred miles. He had a lot of problems but the first was to put those miles between himself and Guildford.

The engine purred through the quiet night, as if joyous at the burst of speed. He remembered the tyres needed air but everything seemed all right, and running at speed wouldn't take much out of the battery, even with the headlights on. The girl kept shifting her position, but didn't try to speak again. She was having a rough time; she deserved a rough time.

The needle kept around sixty-five, much of the road was straight. He slowed down at signposts, never had

to stop.   He wasn't sure that he was going the quickest
way but he was heading in the right direction.

At about half past four, the sky behind him began
to brighten. He drove on, glanced at his watch and
made out the time—ten minutes to five. By five o'clock
the true dawn had come, he couldn't keep the girl as she
was much longer. On the whole run he hadn't passed
a dozen cars ; but country folk were early risers. He
switched off the headlights, then turned a corner, saw
a village some way ahead in a hollow between low hills.
A house was only a hundred yards away, with a board
up in the garden. He slowed down and read : *For
Sale*.

There were no curtains at the windows, the place looked
empty.

" I think we'll have a chat, here," he said, and stopped
outside the gate.

CHAPTER XIV

EMPTY HOUSE

THERE was a drive and a garage, with doors which opened
easily, and the comforting discovery that a copse hid
the house but not the gate from the village. No other
houses were near. Mannering drove the Buick into
the garage, then cut the cord at the girl's wrists and ankles.
She was too stiff to fight; probably she'd lost the will.
There was plenty of room, and he lifted her out, set her
down on her feet and knew that she couldn't walk by
herself—she leaned against the wall of the garage and he
heard the gasp from behind the scarf.

He took a flask of brandy and some slabs of chocolate
out of the dashboard pocket, put them in his own, then
put his arm round Judy's waist and she hobbled out,
leaned against a fence as he closed the garage doors ; no

one would see a car outside an empty house. He kept glancing along the road, fearful of early risers; no one came in sight, no cattle browsed in a meadow behind the house. He helped her to the back door; an old iron garden seat stood by the red brick wall.

He helped her to sit down, then looked at the door, which was solid and had a better lock than most; it wouldn't be as quick and easy to open as he wanted. A big window showed a kitchen, brass taps and a sink. The easy way was to break the window. He picked up a big stone and smashed it just below the catch, and the girl watched him as he pushed the window up.

"You could run away," he said. "You wouldn't get far."

She didn't speak. She seemed to have forgotten everything as she stared at him—and he knew that she had recognised him. She was terrified, stiff with the terror; he couldn't trust her for a moment. He lifted her again, bent her almost double, put her through the window and sat her in the sink. There was room for him to climb through. He scratched his hand on a spike of glass and blood welled up; the night's only injury. He closed the window.

"Come on," he said, lifted her again, set her on her feet and went out of the kitchen. It was empty except for a few oddments and a big cupboard. His feet rang and hers scraped on bare boards. The room beyond was small, an old, broken wicker chair stood against the window and curtains which looked ready to fall to pieces hung behind it. He pulled the curtains gingerly; they didn't tear.

He helped the girl to sit down; she still seemed chilled with fear. Standing behind her, he untied the scarf. When he looked at her, the skin at the corners of her mouth was red, her nose was shiny, there were a few marks where the scarf had been drawn tightly—nothing that mattered. Her wrists were red but she didn't start rubbing them. He took a slab of chocolate out of his pocket, unwrapped it, broke off a piece and handed it to her.

" Hungry ? "

She made no move to take it.

" I'd rather have tea and toast, but why not make the best of this ? " asked Mannering. " Half a mo'." He went into the kitchen, leaving the doors wide open ; he would hear if she made any move. Two cups without handles and two rows of jam-jars stood on a shelf near the sink. The cups were covered with dust, but that wouldn't matter if the water were on. He turned the ' cold ' tap ; water ran at once. He grinned and let it run, went back to the smaller room and said :

" They forgot to turn the water off, don't we have luck ? "

She hadn't moved ; and her eyes looked like green stars as she stared at him. He went back, washed the cups thoroughly, dried the outsides with a handkerchief and took them back, full of water.

" Drink ? "

She swallowed hard, and said something that might have been ' please '. He handed her a cup and helped her to support it. She sipped slowly, but didn't want to stop. He let her drink half the water, then took it away, and drank his own.

" More ? "

She nodded.

When she had finished, he drew back, then deliberately squatted on the floor, both cups by his side. He took out cigarettes.

" Want one ? "

" No—no, thank you."

He lit up, watching her all the time. He'd been wrong in thinking that the other woman was the more beautiful. Odd, that he should think of this girl as beautiful, now— but he did. She would probably never look worse but there was true beauty—as much in her eyes as in her features. The bun of hair at the nape of her neck had come undone, strands hung down untidily. She wore a black swagger coat with two top buttons undone and showing the canary yellow of the familiar jumper. Her hands and her face looked white against the black coat.

She had told Bristow that he had killed Blane and attacked her, and Bristow had believed it. Mannering had never had a better reason for feeling vicious—and he didn't feel mildly angry. He could watch her and not dwell on what she had done so much as why she had done it.

If he let that mood grow stronger he could start getting soft with her, and he couldn't afford to be soft. Already the sharpness of fear had gone from her eyes; he didn't think that it would take much to bring it back, and he started mildly.

"Now we'll have that little talk," he said. "Why did you want to see me last night?"

She didn't answer, and he hadn't expected that she would find her voice quickly. He gave her a few seconds, then hitched himself back so that he leaned against the wall, ankles crossed, cigarette in his hand. "I mean to know," he said. "I mean to find out why you lied to the police, too."

The fear crept back, shining in the vivid green of her eyes. Colour seeped into her cheeks; he had never seen colour in them before. She moved her hands from the wicker arms of the chair and let them rest in her lap.

"Why did you send for me, Judy? Don't be obstinate, I haven't hurt you yet but I'm capable of it." Frightening her too much would do more harm than good. "Just tell me the simple truth, from the beginning. The easy way is to answer my questions. Why did you send for me?"

"I wanted to—talk to you."

"Or did you want to frame me for Blane's murder?"

"No." There was spirit in her voice. "No, it wasn't that, I——"

"Did you kill Blane?"

"*No!*" she cried.

"All right." He could give her a few seconds to get over this surge of agitation. "I'll tell you something. I came to see you, found Blane dead in the chair and you nearly strangled with your own neck band. If I'd been ten minutes or so later you would probably have died."

She didn't speak, but sat upright—he thought that she didn't believe it. She couldn't have known, of course, but why should she reject it automatically?

"It's a fact," he said. "When I saw you on the floor it was one of the bad moments. I worked till I was silly to bring you round. Ribs feel sore this morning?" He asked that casually.

"Why, yes, they did!"

"Where I kept up the pressure for artificial respiration," Mannering said dryly. "I saw you were coming round, hurried for help and ran into trouble. After being left out in the rain all night, I woke up to find that you'd lied to the police and to my wife. Didn't you think she'd had shock enough, finding Blane's dead body?"

He was trying to make the talk seem natural, and was succeeding—much as it had with her mother. *Was* Stella her mother? He was trying to make her think that he hadn't guessed the likely reason for her lies. There was fear in her; fear had made her lie. But fear of what?

"I suppose she had," Judy whispered.

"Now we'll fill in the gaps I don't know about. You came round to find someone else pretending to have pulled you round."

She said: "I—I was lying on the floor, with just blankets over me." The fear was stronger—as if she were afraid that any moment he would realize she was lying.

"I'd brought the blanket. How many men were with you?"

"Two—two," she muttered.

"All right, there was a pair of them. Go back a bit. Tell me exactly what happened after you'd telephoned me. You'd left the front door open and pulled up a chair by the window. What followed?"

She hesitated; then began to speak slowly, as if desperately anxious to convince him. She wasn't bad; just driven by fear.

" I was sitting waiting for you and thought I heard a sound in the hall. I went downstairs, no one was there. I came back, and a man threw—a man threw a cloth over my head. Like you did to-night." She caught her breath. " He tied it round—round my neck. I couldn't breath. I thought——" she broke off, and leaned back, trying to show him how terrified she had been.

Mannering said quietly : " Go on."

She drew a deep breath, seemed to make a physical effort to control herself.

" I don't know how long I was unconscious. I came round on the floor of Mr. Blane's study. He was in— he was in that chair. I knew he was dead. There were two men—they weren't English." She talked like Blane had now, breathlessly and with brief pauses between the sentences. " They wrapped the blanket round me, one of them carried me to my room. They gave me brandy. Then hot coffee."

Into a pause, Mannering asked : " Did you know them ? "

" No. They were strangers. They said that they were friends of Mr. Blane. They said they knew he'd had— he'd had a visit from you, and that you were deadly, that you'd killed others and the police knew and couldn't prove it. They said they'd come too late to save Blane but had saved me. And——"

She paused, but he didn't prompt her. She closed her eyes. All the colour had gone from 'her cheeks again, and he judged it time for the brandy. He stood up, took out his flask and took it across to her ; she watched him through her lashes. He held the flask in front of her, and she took it and swallowed ; she only had one sip, and handed it back. He screwed the cap on, went out with the cups, filled them again and brought them back.

He offered cigarettes after she'd sipped again.

" Thank—thank you." As he lit up and saw the light shine on her eyes, he marvelled that he wasn't viciously angry with her ; but he still felt nothing akin to anger

—more, compassion. He wanted her to believe she was fooling him ; she might talk more freely of other things, about which she could tell the truth.

She drew on the cigarette.

" They told me what to say," she went on slowly, almost fearfully. " They—they convinced me that you had killed Mr. Blane. They *had* been helping me when I came round. They said that the police had never been able to prove you a murderer, that you might get away with yet another, but if I—if I told them what they said, it would settle accounts once and for all. You'd be charged, arrested, and——"

" Hanged for a murder I didn't do."

" I—I thought you had ! "

" Did you ? "

" I was *sure* you had." She spoke as if she knew that he hadn't, was simply justifying herself. " They said they'd been following you all the evening, lost you near Maberley Square, and found your car in time to—in time to bring me round and make you run away."

" And you believed them." His voice was less amiable.

She flared : " Why shouldn't I ? I knew you wanted the jewels. They were gone, the safe was open. I knew you were a jewel merchant, I knew you'd tried to persuade Mr. Blane to sell, it looked——" she broke off, sat up, looked better—the brandy had taken effect. " *Didn't* you kill him ? "

Mannering smiled dryly.

" No. Your boy friends probably did." The men—there'd been two, all right—created another puzzle. If they had gone to Maberley Square, killed Blane and left the girl for dead, why had they come back afterwards and helped her to recover, told her what to say, frightened her into obeying ?

" I—I was sure it was you," the girl went on hurriedly. " I hated you for killing Mr. Blane—not for what you'd done to me. That anyone could kill *him*."

She was close to tears. Could this *be* true ? Could she have been in love with the fat Blane ? That would be almost grotesque. Yet she had been at Blane's beck and call, had been eager, anxious to be ready to serve, fussed over him as a lover would indulge her love.

" It—it's hard to realise that he *is* dead," she said in a husky voice. " I can see him there now—he looked so different in death. I hardly recognised him—I—I've never seen a dead—dead person before."

Now Mannering recognised the truth ; this came from her heart.

She choked back tears, and Mannering waited for them to come, but she went on : " He'd done—he'd done so much to help me, to help others. He was *good*." She meant it—or at least she believed it. " He was just good, I don't believe there is anyone else like him in the world."

She meant that, too.

" Tell me about him," Mannering said.

" It—it's difficult. He was a sick man, stayed home nearly all the time. Only his doctor and one or two close friends ever visited him. He had no time for—for social life, was almost a hermit. Sometimes he would go out for a drive, I'd take him, or his doctor. Sometimes he'd go away for week-ends. David took him out once or twice." She hesitated before saying ' David ', and went deathly pale. Her voice was so low that Mannering could hardly hear the words. " David knew his doctor and visited the house with him once, that's how David and I met."

" I see," Mannering murmured.

" But he—Mr. Blane—hardly thought about himself. He was interested in many charities, had a long list of people he helped. He—he lived to do good."

She knew a different man from the one Blane Mannering had seen.

The girl didn't go on, but the moment for putting on the pressure hadn't quite come. Mannering moved away from the wall and trod his cigarette out on the tiled hearth, watching her closely. He gave her time to recover from the surge of emotion, and then asked quietly :

" How long had you worked for him ? "

" For three years."

" Why did you go to The Manor to-night?" That changed the subject abruptly, bewildered her.

" David didn't want me to stay in the nursing-home," she whispered. Perhaps she knew that David hadn't wanted her where the police could keep up the pressure. " He arrived yesterday afternoon, he'd seen what happened in the newspapers. The police wanted me to stay but they couldn't make me. We left about ten o'clock and went to David's flat but—I just couldn't rest. I wanted to go to mother. Mother had rushed up to London to see me, but had to go back. She can't leave Lady Jane for long. I—I was all right. I just said I *must* go. So David took me. I couldn't sleep, and liked the idea of the drive."

" So it's as simple as that. Who is David ? "

" A—friend."

" No more ? "

" No," she said huskily, fearfully. " Not yet. I think perhaps——"

She didn't finish whatever she was going to say. Her eyes filled with tears again. She didn't fight them ; probably she couldn't. Mannering wasn't surprised. She cried silently but there could be no doubt of her grief ; or of the underlying fear.

He went out of the room, stayed for ten minutes, came back smoking, and tossed a handkerchief into her lap. She was no longer crying. She dabbed at her cheeks and eyes, and blew her nose. Most of her tension would be gone now.

" Thank you." Her voice was muffled.

" Pleasure. Now we'll have the truth." Alarm flared into her eyes at the words, and the steeliness in his voice. " You knew I didn't kill Blane. You knew these men put you up to a lie. How did they force you ? "

She couldn't speak, just stared at Mannering with the terror back in her eyes.

Mannering said harshly :   " What made you do it ?

Whose neck were you hoping to save by putting mine in
its place ? Your own ? " He paused, but she looked as
if she were petrified. " Your own ? " he repeated roughly.
" Or David's. It was David's, wasn't it ? He killed
Blane."

CHAPTER XV

MORE ABOUT KORRA

THE girl just stared at Mannering, with dread in her eyes,
her hands thrust forward as if to fend off some evil thing.
He could have driven her into an admission by working
on her fear, but he didn't want her like this ; he wanted
her to talk. So he went nearer, took her hands, and said
quietly :
" Was it David ? "
" No ! " she cried. " No, it couldn't—David
wouldn't——"
" Do these men exist ? "
" Yes ! Of course they do. They——"
" Did they say David killed Blane ? "
She began to tremble. Mannering put an arm round
her shoulders, meaning to comfort her. He drew the
truth out of her, slowly at first, then more freely. Once
he'd forced the issue, and she knew there was nothing
she could hide, she was almost eager to talk.
David had been jealous of Blane ; David was supposed
to be in the north, she hadn't seen him, but the men had
told her David had killed Blane, and would hang. If
she wanted to save him, she must name Mannering. The
overwhelming passion of her love for David had made
her do it, given her strength to fool the police.
How long could she have kept that up ?
It didn't matter. She was calmer ; but she needed help.
Mannering stood away from her.

" They traded on your fear that David had killed him,"
he said. " Did they offer any proof ? "

" They said—they said they'd seen him at the house."

" I doubt if they'd hurry to tell the police," Mannering
said dryly. " They wanted to frame me—they may
have framed David. Don't take anything for granted."

Judy didn't speak.

" Finding out who did kill Blane means plenty to me,"
Mannering said, easily. " We'll work on this together,
Judy. I've done this kind of job before."

" Oh, I know ! "

" Good. Let's see what we can work out. Why did
you want to see me in the first place ? What did you
hear Blane and me talking about to make you so anxious
to talk to me ? "

He didn't think she would lie again. He thought she
had told the truth about Blane, about everything ; and
there would be time to find out.

She hardly hesitated.

" It was about the jewels and Jacob Korra."

He didn't want her to think that he had an especial
interest in Korra yet, so he spoke easily :

" The jewels were Korra's in the first place, weren't
they ? And Korra wanted them back."

" Yes."

" How did you come to know that ? "

" Mr. Blane told me. I don't think he kept anything
from me, Mr.—Mr. Mannering." She hadn't used his
name before, since she had recognised him. " Mr. Blane
thought that Korra was one of the—of the really bad
men." She spoke half defiantly, as if knowing that she
sounded naive. " Mr. Blane had a very simple philosophy
—a man was either good or bad, and Korra was bad. ᐱHe
knew Korra wanted the jewels back and was determined
never to let him have them. I don't think he would have
sold them to you even if you'd named someone else as
your client, he would have been afraid that Korra was
behind it. He didn't mind letting *Korra* think he might
get them."

So Blane hadn't been above using a little psychological pressure to work on a man's mind—not if he thought that the man was bad. And Blane had appointed himself judge of what was good and what was bad. He had reminded Mannering of a solemn Buddha.

"He had always told me that he thought Korra would try to steal them, might kill for them. The fact that he had them frightened me. There was a burglary, about three weeks ago. Mr. Blane laughed about it, said it was some bungling amateur, but I didn't think he thought so. He was frightened. He's had a weak heart for some years, the doctors warned him that he must avoid exertion and shocks. He had made me afraid of this Korra and of what might happen if Mr. Blane were robbed. I wanted to talk to you about it, to ask you to do everything you could to buy the rubies. I thought that if he sold them there would be no need to worry, that he would have a better chance." The girl paused, and when Mannering didn't speak, added simply: "That's all."

At least he hadn't been fooled by her at the beginning; she had not tricked him into going to Maberley Square. It could be the answer, too; if she were as devoted to Blane as she made out, it was a convincing one. There was a quality of simplicity in her—absent from her mother but very real. Perhaps Blane had taught her something of his own simple philosophy.

"Just that," Mannering said heavily.

"There was no other reason," she said insistently. "I've told you everything now. It's all true."

She hadn't got round to wondering what he would do next. The obvious thing was to take her to a police station; she would talk, when confronted by the police again.

Mannering hadn't a worry in the world; but she had. His danger was past. He could stop at the nearest telephone and call Lorna, tell her there was nothing more to fear.

"What are you going to do ?" Judy asked.

" Get some breakfast," he said lightly, " and think this over."

She seemed satisfied.

" Where are we ? "

" Not far from Yeovil, in Somerset. Where they make gloves ! " The Yeovil police would suit him as well as any. It would be kinder, in the long run, to make her tell her story again quickly : if her David were a killer she would be well rid of him ; if he weren't, the truth would come out. Before or after breakfast ? It couldn't be much after half past six, if it were as late. Judy needed a hot drink, food and rest, and she wouldn't get it until they'd seen the police. " Ready to go on ? "

" Whenever you like." She started to get up. Her cheeks were flushed and her eyes much brighter than when she had arrived—a feverish brightness. " You haven't any aspirins, have you ? "

He had everything in the Buick except aspirins.

" We'll get some," he said, " and a cup of something hot at the first place we come to. Head ache ? "

" Dreadfully."

There wasn't any reason to be surprised at that. He remembered her as he had seen her on the floor, so near death that he had not thought life had a chance. She had thrown off the effects as only the very young could, but it had taken plenty out of her ; and if that weren't enough, there had been the attack at The Manor and the long drive through the night with terror as a companion.

They went out the back way. Mannering left her behind the house and went to the front ; no one was on the road, although in the village, which he could see from the front gate, a man was walking slowly along with a stick in his hand and a dozen cows straggling along behind him. Mannering opened the garage doors and drove the car out. The girl didn't need calling, but joined him before he started to get out.

" You didn't bring my *bag*, did you ? "

He had to laugh.

" Sorry, I forgot ! I——"

She had opened the door and started to get in, stopped and drew back. She took her hand out of her pocket, and her eyes looked brighter. A small bag, an evening bag, was in her hand.

" I'd forgotten this ! " she cried. " David put it in— I left it at his flat last week. I usually have some aspirins in it." She searched, smiled with relief, brought out a little bottle. " This should clear my head—I have a lot of headaches." She got in, shook two tablets on to the palm of her hand and put the bottle away.

" Let's go and get some water," Mannering said. " We can spare a minute." It no longer mattered if they were seen, he'd forgotten that. " I've a better idea—you sit there, I'll get the water."

He switched off the engine and hurried back to the house. But Judy didn't wait, and met him at the corner as he came out with a cup of water. She drank, swallowing the tablets, and a few drops of water fell on to her chin. She wiped them off with her fingers and smiled at him. She looked very young as she put a hand on his arm and they went back to the car.

" Sit back and close your eyes," he advised.

" Oh, I'll be all right. How—how far is it to Yeovil ? "

" I'm not sure. It can't be too far." There might be a transport café open in the village, but Mannering doubted it. There would be a telephone, but it would be wiser— and better for Judy, remember—to see the police first and call Lorna afterwards.

The fact that the worst was over hadn't really sunk in. He found himself smiling as he drove along, slowing down from fifty to thirty through the village and to ten past the cows—and stopped alongside the man with the stick, a youth who was clean-shaven, bright-eyed, wearing unexpectedly clean dungarees.

" Good morning, sir."

" Good morning. How far is it to Yeovil, do you know ? "

" Straight on, sir, you can't miss it, just follow this road for seventeen miles."

" Fine, thanks," said Mannering, and drove on. The girl was sitting up with her eyes wide open, as if she couldn't make herself close them. " Less than half an hour, comfortably. How's the head ? "

" It will be all right," said Judy.

" Good. Care to tell me more about David ? " If he could get her mind off Blane it would help her. Food and a hot drink would help her, too—then the statement and complete relaxation for her, jubilation for him.

The only thing left to do was to find the Korra jewels. He might find them in the search for the two men who had blackmailed Judy. If he found the men first, the Korra jewels could stay for ever with their rightful owners— even their wrongful owners. God, it was good to feel free ! There had been a time when he would have enjoyed——

" David's a doctor," said Judy; he had almost forgotten what he had suggested. " He's spending a year as a *locum*, soon he's going to start on his own. We've known each other for nearly two years. He——" she hesitated, and her voice told Mannering that he'd failed to take her thoughts off Blane; they were right back again. " He wants to marry me. I didn't feel that I could leave Mr. Blane, and David wouldn't listen to my continuing to work." That wasn't surprising, if David knew anything about the influence which Blane had exerted over her. " I almost felt that he was *pleased* when——"

" Forget it," Mannering said briskly. " You weren't in any mood to know what David thought about it." But David might well have been pleased ; might have killed Blane. " Didn't you say he'd been up north ? "

" Yes, as a *locum*. You know, *locum tenens*. He got someone else to act as *locum* for him, to come down." She yawned suddenly, put her hand to her mouth and dropped her bag. " I didn't realise that I was so tired."

" Close your eyes," he said.

She obeyed, and he drove on at a steady fifty. He hoped she wouldn't drop asleep ; he would be reluctant to wake her. The sun was warm already, the sky clear, the countryside fresh in its new cloak of green. He found himself humming softly. Now and again he glanced at the girl. She had gone to sleep; her chin was on her chest, the collar of the coat brushed against her cheek.

It would be a pity to wake her.

It was a quarter past seven when he drove into the outskirts of Yeovil. He'd had time to think beyond the next step towards clearing himself. Those two men had taken the Korra rubies, if Stella Darrow were right, Aristotle Wynne already had the diamonds and the emeralds ; he might be driven by desire for the other set and all the Korra jewels. Aristotle was certainly a man to see. Yeovil was nearer Cornwall than London. Why not drive on ? Judy wouldn't mind, she would be compliant now, and while they were moving she would get the sleep she needed. He could wake her in an hour or so, stop for breakfast and go on to Aristotle. Whatever Judy told the police, they would want to hold Mannering until the Yard gave the ' all clear '—he'd almost forgotten that in the first elation.

He kept glancing at the girl. She didn't move, except with the slight jolting of the car. At Honiton, she was still asleep, and by that time Mannering was beginning to feel really hungry. Judy had had nearly two hours' sleep, enough for the time being. He ought to wake her.

He drove on, but in half an hour she was still sound asleep, and he was so hungry that he was getting light-headed ; he needed a rest from driving. He saw a transport café some way off, pulled into the parking place at one side of it, and switched off the engine. He touched the girl's hand.

" Judy, it's time to wake up."

She didn't stir.

He gripped her hand more tightly, moved it to and fro.

" Wake up, Judy."

She made no move of any kind, gave no sign that she was on the verge of waking. Yet she must have slept during the previous day, even if under drugs. He shook her more vigorously, with a hand at her shoulder.

" Judy ! Wake up ! "

As he shook her, her head lolled to and fro. He watched for any flicker at her eyes, and saw none. He shook her again, and then stopped suddenly. Her face was pale, and cold to the touch. He raised her right eyelid ; the pupil had contracted to a pin-point—as they would with morphia poisoning. Mannering sat still. The morning seemed to go still, also ; as if there were no sound, no one in the world but the two of them. The fear which had stabbed into his mind caused physical hurt.

" Judy ! "

She didn't stir.

Mannering didn't think she ever would, again.

CHAPTER XVI

DEAD WITNESS

A MAN stepped out of the café, which was just a wooden hut with a few brightly coloured advertisements pasted on it, and a long window covered with advertising stickers, and walked towards Mannering. He was short, wore a pair of dirty overalls, a short-sleeved khaki shirt and a peak cap. He needed a shave ; the sun shone on stubble that was nearly as yellow as corn. He nodded to Mannering.

" Up early, mate ? "

" Catching the worm," Mannering said mechanically.

The man grinned and passed by. Mannering watched him in the driving-mirror ; he climbed into a small van at the far end of the parking space, and drove off away from Honiton. Mannering put his hand back on Judy's. He had felt her pulse and found that it was still and couldn't believe it. He felt cold ; inwardly, not out-wardly. Her hand felt cold, too—that was imagination, it must be. He searched for the pulse again, with his finger, pressed gently against the slender wrist and felt nothing ; nothing.

He watched her lips.

They were lovely lips, if pale, and they were set so still that they might have belonged to a wax model ; so might her delicately turned nostrils; and her eyes were also still.

He said aloud, hoarsely : " No."

He took a small mirror out of the dashboard pocket and held it in front of her nose and mouth ; there was no misting over. She was warm and she was still, there was no life left in her.

At the house, she had been not only alive but vital ; distressed and yet eager with new hope, beautiful, with life in front of her and what might well have been the first great tragedy of her life also in the past. Now, there was death.

" No ! " Mannering exclaimed. " It can't be true."

His mind rejected it at the same time as he knew that it was true, that Judy Darrow was dead. She had stepped into the car willingly this time, and talked almost brightly. Mannering had gone for the water, and her eyes had said ' thanks ' as she swallowed the tablets and drank. Then she had talked for a while, yawned, slept and—died.

Mannering turned the ignition key, slowly. He was hot, now, and very dry, but he couldn't stay here for food. He couldn't leave the girl, he had to be sure that he was right about her. That burned into his mind—the hope that he was wrong. Could this be a collapse ? A form of catalepsy ? Victims of that who looked dead were alive ; doctors could be fooled. He must get her to a doctor.

He didn't drive off. The engine ticked over smoothly. A milk lorry slowed down as it approached the café, turned in, and pulled up behind him. The driver and his mate got down and passed Mannering, lighting cigarettes without looking at him. They went inside.

He must take her to a doctor but he had to weigh this
up first. Her death changed, worsened, everything;
might be deadly to him. Judy had told the police her
story of his killing Blane and attempt to kill her. Now
she sat beside him—dead. He pictured Bristow's face;
Farley's; a judge's and the jury's. There would only be one
answer to the questions they would ask. If she were
dead, he was within an ace of the gallows.

How had she died ?

He didn't need to think. She had been alert and
live before the headache had made her search for aspirins.
She had said she often took them; two aspirins would
ease pain, might induce sleep, but wouldn't kill; so there
had been something else in those tablets.

Her David was a doctor.

Her David had given her the bag before they had left
his flat, she had left it there a week ago.

Mannering did not know David's other name, knew
him only as a shadowy figure and an impatient voice.
But if the tablets had killed her, her David had a lot to
answer for—but not so urgently as Mannering, who had
to explain how it was that the chief witness, the damning
witness against him had died by his side.

Who else was there to say that she had brought the
bag from David's flat ? No one. Who could say that
David had given it to her ? No one. If the man had
meant her to take one of these and die, then he would
have been careful to wipe the glass tube of prints. Mannering could tell the story to a disbelieving Bristow, David
would be questioned and would deny it all. He would
have to admit that he had gone to The Manor—and then
he would tell his story, of the kidnapped girl and the
borrowed M.G. The more Mannering added up, the
greater the total of evidence against him.

What should he do ?

Get the girl to a doctor, yes—but after that, what ?

Two men had brought her round at Maberley Square,
David—surely it was David !—had given her poisoned
tablets instead of aspirin. The two men had wanted the

Korra rubies, so Mannering was back on that trail—and the next clue was Aristotle Wynne.

He had set out for Aristotle Wynne and was nearer him than London.

Mannering put the car in gear and moved off. Two trucks drew up, and waited for him to drive out. He waved acknowledgment and the drivers seemed to stare at Judy. They would think that she was asleep. He had to be sure that she was dead ; no, that wasn't it, he was sure—he had to hear someone else say so.

He had saved her life once when it had seemed lost, there must be a chance. He was heading south-west, stopped, swung round and went towards Honiton, the nearest town and the nearest hospital. He still wasn't sure what to do. If he took her into the hospital there would be countless questions, he would be detained—oh, forget it, he couldn't take her in. At best he could take her to the door, lift her out of the car and leave her ; she would get attention then, but he wouldn't know what the doctors thought.

He reached the outskirts of the straggling Devon town, inquired for the hospital, and a middle-aged woman who directed him glanced at Judy and said how ill she looked.

" Yes," said Mannering. " I can't understand it."

He didn't want to drive into the hospital grounds, but it had to be done. The air of unreality was with him all the time. Two nurses looked out of a window, another stood with her back to it, a sleepy porter was on duty just inside the entrance, and leaned forward as Mannering stopped. Mannering got out, and the man stood up and came to the head of the steps.

" Can I help you ? "

Mannering didn't look at him, did not want his face to be seen clearly ; but it had been. He had to take his chance ; the porter couldn't stop him from getting away, could only send a warning to the police. They would have Mannering's description in the disguise and a description of the car—the police would have him within an hour. He shouldn't have come here. He didn't slacken his efforts as he lifted the girl out of the car. He had to make sure that she had help, even though he knew that nothing could help her.

" *She* looks bad," the porter said.

" Yes. Bad for me, too. Gave her a lift, and she did this. Couldn't wake her." Mannering spoke jerkily. " I'm in a hurry, got to get to London early this afternoon." At least that would mislead and might give him a little more time. " My name's Rasen—Rasen. The King's Head, Putney, will find me." He hardly knew what he was saying. " Make sure she sees a doctor straight away, won't you ? "

" Here, that isn't—— "

Mannering lifted the girl, put her against the porter who had to hold her or let her fall.

" Sorry, can't stay. Desperate hurry." Mannering swung round to the car. The porter called out to him but he didn't look back. He had left the engine running, he was out of the porter's sight within sixty seconds, and the man could never be sure whether he had turned towards London or not.

Mannering made for the road he had come from—the road to Cornwall. He forced himself to keep down to thirty miles an hour in Honiton, then put his foot down. He was calculating carefully. Say ten minutes for the porter to get the girl into an examination room and call the doctor ; five for the doctor to arrive, at most ; say another five before he was sure that the girl was dead. Five to get to a telephone and talk to the police, ten for the police to arrive, ten more before they got the story straight. Would it happen any faster than that ? Ten —fifteen—twenty—thirty—forty minutes. To be on the safe side, say half an hour. After that, better assume that the call for the Buick would have been sent out. But it wouldn't reach the country police for a while although it would be picked up by police patrol cars. The truth was simple ; he should be out of the Buick within half an hour; forty minutes at the very outside.

He went through several villages and didn't notice the names. In two he saw the cottage with the words *Devon Constabulary* outside, but he saw no sign of a policeman. He kept looking at his watch; zero hour was nine o'clock. What should he take out of the car? The tool kit, the chocolate, the make-up box, and he might be wise to take the A.A. book, too. There was no need to load himself with too many things, it would restrict his movement.

He already had the gun; Stella Darrow's gun. Stella Darrow was going to get a shock that would really break through her poise.

Mannering turned off the main road at nine o'clock exactly, drove towards a copse which looked thick and friendly. When he reached it, he found that on the fringe the beech and birch trees were sparse and there was plenty of room to drive among them even with the big car. He went off the road, twisted and turned until the road was out of sight, and then came across a path which was more than just a path; cars or lorries had flattened out the ground, there was damp mud on top; why had vehicles made this road? Nothing suggested that it had been used recently; Mannering turned further from the road and drove steadily.

The copse came to an end abruptly; immediately ahead was a stone quarry, obviously no longer being worked. There were no buildings, no sheds, just the gaping hole in the hillside, and trees round three sides but empty land on the other. He got out, took the chocolate, make-up box and the A.A. book, strapped box and book together and hung it over his shoulder, and put the chocolate in his pocket. Then he hesitated, wondering whether to push the car over. It would be seen down there by anyone who happened along, just as easily as if he left it where it was.

He left it, and walked among the trees, alert, listening for others who might be about.

He could take it for granted that the police were on the look-out, and that they had his description; or a des-

cription. The porter would probably be vague about
the colour of his brown tweed suit, but if he could get
hold of a dark-coloured one it would give him a long
respite.

He had twenty-three pounds in his pocket, and a few
shillings. That wouldn't last for long. It didn't need
to last long. Once the Yard and the Honiton police
compared notes the manhunt would become so fierce
that it would kill his chance of staying free. If he kept
free long enough to tackle Aristotle Wynne he would
be lucky; twenty-four hours of freedom were unlikely,
forty-eight would be a miracle—unless he just bought
food and hid away. Where would that get him? Not
to the two men and not to the Korra jewels. He had to
see Wynne, his one hope of information about Korra,
and he hadn't the slightest idea whether the man whom
Blane had called Arry would have any answers that
mattered.

He stayed for ten minutes among the trees, seeing
the movements of birds and the scurrying of rabbits.
A stoat appeared, sniffing the air, then disappeared.
Two rats came out of thick undergrowth to sun themselves, frisked and sparred with each other. The sweet
song of a blackbird seemed to rise higher and higher;
pigeons at the top of an old, spreading oak tree cooed
and were answered.

No human being appeared.

Mannering went back to the car, opened all the doors,
rested the make-up case mirror against the windscreen
where it lodged against the wiper arms, then sat on the
back seat. The light was good. He cleaned off the
grease-paint with cotton wool soaked in spirit, and
began from scratch. He needed perfection and that
meant he needed time. With each stage of the make-
up he stopped, got out of the car and looked round;
no one appeared to be watching, there were the familiar
sounds of the woods, birds flew swiftly and cast their
shadows, early wasps and mosquitoes hummed and hovered,
flies wove their unending, invisible webs.

At each stage, too, he paused to inspect himself. At first, he had been John Mannering with his cheeks a little plumper than usual. His face began to change and his expression with it. As he worked in the grease-paint, cut his hair with a pair of hand clippers, pushed a special soft-setting cement into his nostrils, to make his nose fuller ; a different man seemed to be looking at himself in the mirror. A bleach for the hair, now short at his temples and the nape of his neck, took the colour out and made it grey. He looked older ; a man in the middle fifties. At the fourth stage he paused longer than before and scrutinised himself from every angle, using a hand-mirror to see the back of his head—the back of a head could give him away almost as quickly as his face. The way he had clipped his hair would do.

He took thin rubber casing from the case and worked it over his teeth with infinite care ; when it was on his teeth looked yellow, one had a silver top. He grinned broadly to get the proper effect, and was satisfied.

He put everything back in the case and slung it over his shoulder again. If he left it here and the car were discovered, the police would know that he had made up. Bristow would guess, anyhow, but trifling precautions mattered.

Now his chief worry was his clothes. There was nothing he could do about that yet. He closed the doors of the car, turned and walked away.

CHAPTER XVII

POLGISSY

A POLICEMAN with a spiked helmet cycled along the narrow street of Polgissy, nodding to passers-by, several of whom had to step off the road and on to the yard wide pavement to let him pass. There was scarcely room here for two cars—even small cars—to pass. The policeman stopped at crossroads so narrow that only a really midget car could turn any corner without reversing at least once. The sun shone warmly on slate roofs, whitewashed walls here and there a modern shop front, on flagstones, the cobbled road surface and the tiny shops themselves.

At the crossroads were four shops—including an off-licence for the sale of wines and spirits, beer and cider to customers who had no time to bend their necks to get beneath the low lintel of the entrance to the *Crossways Inn*, an old, crooked gabled building close by. The inn had one window of the bottle glass which had first been put in three hundred and eleven years ago—when Polgissy had already been a fishing village with a long history. Then smugglers had trundled their barrels or pulled their crates and kegs and boxes on sleds across the cobbles, and many a Preventative man's eye had been closed while the owner was wide awake. Then, the fishing boats had gone out at dawn and often come back at dawn, unloading their catch on the quay behind the *Crossways Inn*.

The boats still went out, but were larger and not wholly dependent on sail. The fish were still landed on the quay where the stones were worn smooth by slapping fish down, after weighing, ready for market and the eager housewives. Some of the fishermen looked as if they had been ready to slake their thirst after the tang of the salt sea spray in the inn as long ago as it had been built; but some were young.

From the crossroads one could see the mouth of the Pol River, the masts of the boats, the gulls hovering and calling small craft moving sluggishly towards the open sea, beyond the two stone-built harbours.

The policeman watched them for a moment, then leaned his bicycle against a stone wall and looked at the grocery and provision shop opposite the off-licence, the confectionery and tobacco shop on another corner—

and finally moved towards the fourth shop, which looked
older than any of the others. It had a big oak beam,
uneven in shape, as a fascia board, and oak beams at
the sides of the windows. Inside, it looked dark. The
window was a famous one in Polgissy—more holiday-
makers and tourists stopped there and were persuaded to
buy than anywhere else in the little village.

Yet not all the goods offered were trinkets or hand-
made Cornish pottery or polished rock ashtrays, with
or without seagulls for decoration. Some of the jewellery
had come from Birmingham but some was old ; collectors
from London had rubbed their eyes with astonishment
at the sight of a priceless vase among the pottery, or a
pendant, which had once adorned a victim of the French
Revolution, among the second-hand jewellery offered for
sale.

Aristotle Wynne, who owned the shop, marked the price
of everything on show. That morning the policeman
looked at a pair of diamond ear-rings, marked £1,100,
and at others priced from a few shillings upwards on
the same shelf. The policeman, a young, brown-faced
and keen-eyed man, grinned and wondered what old
Arry would be up to next, ducked his head so that the
spike on his helmet seemed as if it were lowered for a
charge, and went inside.

Wynne was behind the only counter, a glass show-case,
a tall, thin, melancholy-looking man—more solemn,
perhaps, than melancholy, with a bedraggled moustache
which drooped almost to his chin, wrinkled but weather-
beaten skin, mournful brown eyes behind *pince-nez*.
He had a long neck and a prominent Adam's apple. Many
of the older residents of Polgissy swore that while in the
shop they had never seen him wearing anything different
from the velveteen smoking jacket of wine red, the
winged collar and cravat, and the baggy grey trousers.
Out in his little boat or standing at the quayside with
his line and bait in the water, Arry Wynne wore a blue
jersey and everything else, like the rest of them.

A tall man, corpulent, hair very grey at the sides and

the back of the neck, with florid, fat cheeks and a rather bulbous nose was looking at a tray of jewellery, and Wynne watched him closely until the policeman came in, his big frame darkening the shop while he was at the doorway ; the shop was dark enough without that.

" 'Morning, Arry."

" Why, good evening, Silas," said Aristotle Wynne, and smiled a greeting. " What can I do for you this evening ? "

" Don't let me interrupt business," said P.C. Silas Fowey, with a grin.

Mannering, the customer, glanced up and waved a hand.

" I'm in no hurry," he said, " no hurry at all." His voice had a faintly north-country accent. He wore a loose-fitting Norfolk jacket and a pair of grey flannel trousers which fitted a little tightly at the waist. Both looked as if he had worn them for years ; no one would have guessed that he had bought them at St. Austell a few hours ago—the coat at one secondhand dealer's shop, the trousers at another. " Mr. Wynne has some wonderful jewels here, wonderful."

" You're not the first to say so," said P.C. Fowey. " Well, if you're not in a hurry, I'll have a word with Mr. Wynne. Arry, you've met a lot of these big jewel merchants, haven't you—the topnotchers, I mean. London and all that."

" Many of them, Silas."

" This Mannering, now," said Fowey, and took a folded newspaper from his pocket, " have you ever met him ? "

" The man with his photograph in all the papers," said Wynne, and looked more melancholy than ever. " Well, in a way I have and in a way I haven't."

Mannering, a yard away from him, didn't look up.

" Now I wonder what you mean by that ? " asked Fowey.

" It's simple enough, Silas. I've been into his shop, a very fine shop he has—Quinns, you may have read about it. A *very* fine shop, and Mr. Mannering has a wonderful reputation. I've seen him each time but haven't spoken to him. I didn't feel that I was justified and he has an excellent staff. So I've seen him, been as close to him as I have to this gentleman here, but I couldn't say I've *met* him."

" But you'd recognise him."

" Oh, I'd *recognise* him in a flash."

" Well, just keep your eyes open," said Fowey. " We think he was at Honiton this morning. I won't go into any details but it was a nasty business, very nasty. A girl died. He told a porter at the hospital he was going to London, but that could have been to fool the man—he *could* have come down this way. Wouldn't be the first on the run to try to hide away with the holiday crowds, would he ? "

" He certainly wouldn't, Silas."

" So if you see him, even if you see anyone who *might* be him, just tip me the wink, Arry, won't you ? "

" Most certainly I will."

To refresh Aristotle Wynne's memory, Fowey showed him the photograph in the *Record*—a good likeness—then folded it carefully, wished them both good evening, and went on his way. Again the shop became very dark as he passed through the doorway. Aristotle Wynne stood with both frail hands on the glass top of the showcase, and as Fowey moved off on his bicycle, he said sardonically :

" Just tip me the *wink*. Why don't the young people use our language properly ? Don't you think it's a pity that our beautiful language is misused so often, sir ? "

Mannering looked up and grinned.

" Aye, but I've heard southerners say that us Yorkshire folk couldn't talk English if we tried."

" Dialect is one thing, slang quite another," said Aristotle Wynne, and smiled as if to make sure that the other was in no way affronted. " What do you think of that ruby set in diamonds ? A beautiful thing, isn't it ? "

" Perfect," agreed Mannering bluffly. " Never seen a better, but I don't care for rubies myself. Never have.

Even when I had the shop I'd let rubies go. It isn't that
I'm superstitious, either."

"Now I'm very different," Aristotle said. "Rubies
have always appealed to me, sir, they seem to *live* more
than other stones—as if they're made of crystalised
blood."

"Aye, I can see what you mean. Perhaps that's one
of the reasons why I've never had much time for them.
But that's a beauty," Mannering repeated. "I will say
I didn't expect to find jewellery of this quality down here,
Mr. Wynne. Mind if I come and look round again in
the morning?"

"By all means, you're welcome, as welcome as could
be," said Aristotle. "I shall be open at half past nine
and here myself."

"Aren't you here all the time?"

"No, I go away a great deal," said Wynne. "To
sales and other dealers, it's as much a hobby as a business
with me. I've a good assistant, though, very good in-
deed, *very* reliable. I expect to be away the day after
tomorrow, I'll tell her you may come in. Just browse as
long as you like, Mr——"

"Gibson's my name."

"Mr. Gibson," said Aristotle Wynne. "You'll excuse
me for a few minutes now, won't you, I have to go to
the back of the shop. There's a little repair job to
finish."

"Always at it," grinned Mannering. "Don't I know
what it's like! Big mistake, I always said, to live over
the shop, too. I did all my life and I haven't stopped
regretting it. They come at all hours, think we don't
know what it's like to have a few hours off. Don't you
find that?"

"It *can* be a nuisance," agreed Aristotle Wynne, "but
I can see the caller from my sitting-room window, if
I want to open the door I do, if I don't I just don't hear
the bell." He gave his melancholy smile which for a
moment became almost mischievous. "If you want me,
just call out."

"I won't worry you," promised Mannering.

Aristotle Wynne, who lived over his shop, disappeared through a small doorway at the back, and a light went on. Mannering could see a flight of narrow stairs beyond the doorway; and wondered what other crooked stair-cases and twisting passage ways there were above the shop, which was probably as old as the *Crossways Inn*. Later in the night, he would find out. He moved about, and marvelled at the goods which Wynne had to offer. The old man's many trips out of Polgissy were to sell as well as to buy, he couldn't hope to dispose of much of his stock to visitors or the nine hundred odd residents of the fishing village.

As he picked up an old Genoese casket of hand-beaten silver, Mannering wasn't worrying about Wynne's business, but of the news which the young Silas had given him.

He had known it was true, but until then, had fought against believing it.

Judy was dead.

Judy, who had set him on the run and then could have cleared him, had drawn the noose tighter round his neck. Or her David had. Mannering had spent a lot of time thinking of her David. There might come a time when he would have to know more about the youth, but that would have to come later; probably when he was behind bars, held on remand.

It wasn't easy to convince himself that he would be able to avoid a charge; it would have been folly to take it for granted that he would. If he had a chance to get at the truth, it would be here, above the shop or below it; there was sure to be a cellar, probably a strong-room.

He could hear Wynne working, and took his time examining the wall fixtures. If Wynne were as cunning as he might well be, then any entrance to a strong-room might be from the shop, concealed behind a fixture. Mannering peered and probed, always with some odd-ments in his hand, until he heard Wynne get up. He went back to the show-case.

"Tell you one thing you might have, Mr. Wynne, just a trifle—can't afford any of these, as I told you. Do you happen to have a really cheap *watch*?"

"Watch?" echoed Wynne. "Well, I have several that are very good value, but cheap——"

"Busted mine today," Mannéring said, "I can't afford to get a good one, only want it until I can get this one repaired. While I'm on holiday, that is. I can repair it myself when I get back, needs one or two parts. Something about a quid, say."

"Well, why not borrow one of these?" asked Wynne promptly. "The lowest-priced one I have is four pounds ten, I won't keep the cheap new stuff, but if you'd like to borrow one while I'm here you can, gladly."

"Well, I don't like to——"

"I know a man I can trust," said Wynne almost drearily, "It would be a pleasure. A pity to spoil your holiday by having something cheap and nasty to look at every time you want to tell the time." He took an old silver turnip watch from the case and held it out.

"Only four pounds ten, for *that*?" Mannering took it. "It's worth twice as much, Mr. Wynne."

"I bought it cheaply at a sale," said Wynne. "If you care to buy it, I'd accept three pounds ten. Take it for now, Mr. Gibson. If you decide to buy it before you leave, I'll be happy, if you want to give it me back I'll be just as happy. You'll have to excuse me now, I must shut up the shop."

"On my way," said Mannering, and pocketed the watch. "That's very generous. If I save enough out of my expenses, I'll buy it with pleasure. Good night—sure you won't mind if I look in tomorrow? Fascinates me, this stuff does."

"How well I know what you mean," said Aristotle Wynne. "It has been a pleasure to talk to someone who knows what he's talking about. Until tomorrow, then."

Mannering went out, waved, and walked along the street leading to the quay. There were over two hours

of daylight left, it was just six o'clock. He forced thought
of Judy away, concentrated on Aristotle Wynne, the
man with the generous impulses, the man with a fortune
in his poky little shop where chance trade was negligible
but who, as far as Mannering could tell, had nothing
that was stolen. His first suspicion that Wynne was a
fence in a big way and felt safe with the stuff down here
was probably wrong.

He didn't dislike Wynne; didn't see him as a thief
—an employer of murderers; only as a man who might
lead to Korra.

Mannering watched the fishermen for ten minutes,
was mildly amused by two small boys standing on the
quayside with string dangling from bamboo sticks, probably
with a pin at the end, then turned back. The streets of
Polgissy were so narrow, especially near the *Crossways
Inn*, that the roofs seemed almost to touch. They didn't,
of course; there were six or seven feet between them.
But the roof of the inn seemed, from here, to be only
an arm's length from the roof of the building where
Wynne had his shop. In the bedroom he had taken at
the inn, Mannering could stand at the window and look
at the net curtains of a window on the second floor above
the shop.

He wasn't quite sure of the best way in but he thought
it would be from the top.

He turned into the *Crossways Inn*. The long saloon
bar, where a fire had been burning in a huge hearth for
several hours, was on the right; the stairs on the left.
It was gloomy enough inside for him to go in and order
a whisky and soda and drink it without any fear of being
scrutinised too closely. Good though the disguise was,
he still couldn't take chances. Three people stood at
the bar, a young couple sat in the window, their faces
tinged green by the light coming through the bottle
glass. Mine host, a thin man with little hair, was busy
behind the bar with a polishing cloth and glasses. Mannering stood near him as he drank, exchanged polite
remarks with the others, and was wondering whether to

offer them a drink when the door opened and Silas the Constable came in. He wore a blue jersey with a roll neck and a pair of flannels, and his spiked helmet had hidden a fine mass of glossy black hair. He joined the three at the bar, gave Mannering a hearty good evening, and made Mannering decide not to stay long. Mannering took a long time over his drink, fighting against the nervousness which the closeness of a policeman always created for the Baron.

He had nearly finished when the door opened again, and Josh Larraby came in.

CHAPTER XVIII

VISITOR

Josh hesitated as the door swung behind him, looked round as any stranger would when coming into an unfamiliar bar, smiled as if satisfied, went across to the fire and rubbed his hands briskly. His hair looked pinky white in the firelight, his chubby face looked cold and red. He wore a thick muffler and a heavy coat. He turned to the bar, stood next to Mannering and glanced at him but showed no special interest—not even the momentary start he would have given had he known who it was.

" Evening, sir," said mine host. " What's for you ? "

" A whisky, I think," said Larraby, loosening his muffler. " I think I could even manage a double. And soda."

" Yes, sir." The manager turned his back and turned the tap of the measure, whisky came from the bottle upside down in its wall bracket.

Larraby rubbed his hands again.

" Getting cold outside."

" Aye, it is that," Mannering said, and his voice was

slightly more north country than it had been with Wynne. He hadn't got over the shock yet.

" You're nearly empty," said Larraby. " Care for another, sir ? "

" Well——"

" I'm sure you would," said Larraby. " Give this gentleman the same as he had before, please." He was brisker than the Larraby of Quinns, yet curiously gentle, and his face was that of a cherub.

The drinks arrived, they looked at each other face to face, and still Larraby showed no sign of recognition, was just talking to a stranger.   Mannering felt better.

" Your very good health, sir."

" And yours, I will say." Mannering drank, no one took any notice of them, they chatted idly for five minutes, and Larraby finished his drink. " Have another," said Mannering, " and let's take it over by the fire, shall we ? "

" You're very kind," said Larraby.

They sat at a small table near the fire, Mannering with his back to the others in the room, Larraby looking at them ; and Larraby didn't know that one was a local policeman.   Larraby must have moved fast to get down here, and must have slipped the police—which probably meant that they would be on the look-out for him.   Bristow would take every possible step, would assume that Larraby knew where Mannering was.   Larraby may have made sure that he hadn't been followed, but there might be a call out for him—not only in London but in the south-west.

It wouldn't be safe to stay long with Larraby, but—why had he come ?

Larraby now seemed to have all the time in the world. Mannering made his drink last, Larraby took much longer over his second.   It was odd for Mannering to look into a face he knew almost as well as his own, and be taken for a stranger.   He would have relished it but for the new risk which Larraby brought ; the darkening shadow of danger.

Was the policeman paying him special attention, or were his darting glances free of real interest ? Mannering turned the conversation—he was staying at the *Crossways Inn*, was Larraby ?   Larraby said that he wasn't yet certain, he might have to go on a bit further—he was to meet a friend here later.

Was that true or an excuse for not being sure ?

" It's comfortable," Mannering said, " very comfortable, in my room leastways." He glanced up, saw that the policeman was looking the other way, dabbed his finger in the wet ring on the table caused by his glass, and traced a number with it—8. He finished and looked straight into Larraby's eyes.

Larraby lost all expression, looked absolutely blank—his way of showing his shock.

" If you don't go on, I'll see you again," Mannering said. He stood up, wished the others a general cheerio, and went out. He didn't look back at Larraby. He felt hot as he climbed the stone steps, so narrow that his arms brushed the walls on either side, so worn that he had to tread carefully. The second flight was of wood, and covered with hair-carpet. He reached the top landing ; there were two rooms and a bathroom—Rooms 7 and 8. He didn't know whether 7 was occupied ; he wasn't sure whether to hope that Larraby would book it.

The policeman was still downstairs ; if Larraby's face had meant anything to the man, would he have stayed so long ?   Had there been time for Bristow to circulate a photograph of the manager of Quinns ? A photograph was hardly necessary, Larraby was the easiest man in the world to recognise from a description.

What *had* brought him ?

Why not forget the danger, assess the advantages ? There were plenty. Larraby would have money with him, and Mannering needed more. Larraby would be able to start inquiries about Judy's David—and Larraby might have news of Korra.

Mannering switched on an electric fire. The window-frame rattled in the wind. He went to the window and

looked out at the darkened room opposite, the room two
floors above Wynne's shop. He could see the shop door
and its street window; he could also see the big bay
window immediately above it, the curtains were parted,
showing a window-seat covered with red plush. Sitting
there, Wynne could look down at his own front door and
identify any callers.

Mannering felt on edge, anxiety fed by eagerness.
Larraby couldn't have misunderstood that figure 8.
Couldn't he? It might have meant eight o'clock. It
was now seven; an hour waiting and hoping that Larraby
would tap at the door was the last thing Mannering
wanted.

He heard boards creak outside; he must remember
that boards in these old buildings often creaked, they
would at Aristotle Wynne's. He turned towards the
door, and there was a light tap.

He stood still.

Larraby opened the door and stepped inside.

He closed the door quietly, then stood for a moment,
studying Mannering, and smiling; the smile broadened
the longer he stood there. Then he moved forward.

" I wouldn't have known if we'd been together all day,"
he said. " It's superlative ! "

Mannering grinned. " I've had enough practice. You
gave me plenty to think about, Josh. Who knows you've
come up here ? "

" I'm using the cloakroom, officially," Josh said. " It's
on two floors below, that'll give me five minutes. I'm
not sure that I ought to book that room across the landing
it's free, but——"

" Don't Josh."

" I thought you'd say that. I gave Bristow's men the
slip easily enough but they might have sent a call out.
Not that they could pull me in," Larraby went on, " but
once Bristow knows I've vanished he'll guess I've come
to see you. Shall I just talk Mr.——" he paused—
" Gibson."

" Yes, Josh."

Larraby began to talk, taking a small package out of
his breast pocket as he did so. He kept his voice low,
and he was as concious of the risk as Mannering.

"Mrs. M. and I guessed you would come down here,
after last night," Larraby said. "It was worth a chance,
anyway. I tried two pubs before this one. As far as
we know, Bristow hasn't got this address—he certainly
didn't know the Surrey one, until he heard what had
happened." Larraby didn't give Mannering time to
comment, but went on: "Here's a hundred pounds,
and Mrs. M. has worked out a code advertisement for
the *Gazette* in case you need any more, you can have it
sent to any post office, of course." He put the package
down on the bed. "I'll just run over the rest and if
you think we ought to have a longer talk, we'll fix something. Chittering told us about Judy Darrow, down at
Honiton. The police weren't long getting on to who
she was, the news was at the Yard by half past nine. He
told us plenty more, too, Mr. Mannering, and most of
it's bad. You can guess how bad."

Mannering nodded.

"We know about the call on Mrs. Darrow at The
Manor," Larraby said, "but don't know what she said
to the police, I can't tell you a thing about her. Soon
after you took the girl away, the young man raised the
alarm. Bristow himself was at Melbury at four o'clock
this morning."

"He would be. What about the boy, Josh?"

"David Graham?"

"So he's David Graham," Mannering said heavily.

Larraby looked puzzled.

"I don't know much about him, he doesn't seem to
come in it, except by accident. He's been going with
Judy for a couple of years—he's just been registered as
a doctor and has been a *locum tenens* up at Bradford for a
few weeks. What makes you interested in him?"

"He killed the girl."

"He killed——" began Larraby, and then broke off.
He didn't argue or throw doubts, just accepted it.

" Do you know what poison it was ? "

" Morphia, according to Chittering," Larraby said. " The boy would have access to drugs, of *course*." He paused. " What would you like me to do about him ? "

" Just dig into his background. Get Chittering to help if he will——"

" Oh, he will."

" Three people who don't think I've turned murderer," Mannering said. " Don't *do* a thing, don't let the police get any idea that you suspect David Graham, we might have to tackle him ourselves. But find out everything you can about him, especially his friends, anyone he mixes with—oh, you don't need telling what to do, Josh, we need as complete a dossier as we can get. And try to trace a Jacob Korra Melano."

" Melano ? " echoed Larraby.

" Korra's real name."

" I won't lose a minute," Josh promised quietly. " Now I really ought to go, I've been away——"

He stopped abruptly, and turned round. There were footsteps on the creaky wooden stairs ; heavy footsteps, more like a man's than a woman's.

CHAPTER XIX

NEWS

LARRABY didn't need telling what to do. He moved swiftly behind the door and stood with his back to the wall. The footsteps drew nearer, were soon on the little landing. Would the policeman walk so heavily ? The boards creaked, and there was a tap at the door.

" Who's that ? " called Mannering.

" Just the maid, sir, come to turn the bed down," a woman said breathlessly.

" Oh." The ordinary things were always the most

likely. "Don't worry just now, I'm changing. I'll do it."

"Well, sir, there's the *towels*."

"Leave them on that table outside, will you? You can come again in ten minutes, if you want to."

"Well, there's no need, if you don't mind turning the bed down, sir."

"I don't mind a bit," Mannering said.

The woman moved off, and every footstep suggested that she found walking a trial; going down the stairs, she seemed to drop her full weight on every tread.

"Is that everything, Mr. Mannering?"

"Tell Mrs. Mannering there's good reason to think Wynne knows a lot." There wasn't—but it would reassure Lorna. From the moment she had seen Blane's body, Lorna must have been in torment. It was less than forty-eight hours since he had seen her; even to him, it seemed an age. "And tell her David Graham gives us another line, so we've plenty to work on."

"I'll do that. Just one other thing, sir."

"Yes?"

"How far have you trusted Daniel Farley?" Larraby asked, and he seemed uneasy. "He called at the flat this morning, very early. Mrs. Mannering said that he insisted that if she could get a message to you, she should persuade you to give yourself up. He said that he had not yet told the police of your visit to him, but that there were limits to withholding information and he was very worried. *He* knows about this place, doesn't he?"

"What time did you leave London?"

"Just after eleven—I borrowed a friend's motor-bike."

"Some travelling, Josh! And as far as you know, Bristow didn't know about Polgissy then."

"No."

"We'll have to hope that Farley squared his conscience a bit longer," Mannering said. "All right, Josh, and thanks—more than thanks." He shook hands. "Tell

Mrs. Webber I'll be coming for some more fish and chips before long."

" Ah," said Larraby. " I've never known a woman who could fry fish and chips like her. More to the point, Mr. Mannering, I've tucked the motor-bicycle away in an old barn just on the other side of the bridge. You can't miss it, but be careful of the ditch. There's a bit of old sacking and some hay over the bike. The tank's full, it's all okay."

" Wonderful, Josh."

" I'll get off, now," Larraby said. " God be with you, Mr. Mannering."

Mannering stood at the open door, saw Larraby going down, keeping close to the wall, making hardly a sound until he reached the landing below. Mannering went back into the room, closed the door, sat on the bed and untied the package. The pound notes inside were all old, probably taken from Quinns, no one could trace them. Josh would look after details like that—and he had taken the right risk. He would probably travel through the night and reach London in the early hours. Lorna would have news before morning.

Mannering put some of the notes into his wallet, folded others and tucked them into his pockets, screwed up the brown paper and tossed it into the waste-paper basket by the fireplace.

It was half past seven. Dinner was served between seven and eight, he would soon have to go, but he must make time for one urgent job. Chittering of the *Record* was probably at his desk, writing up his stories for the early editions ; he liked to be at the office between seven and eight. Chittering was a friend in the right place.

Mannering went downstairs. The only telephone he had seen was a prepayment one outside the cloakroom door on the first floor. A heavy, shapeless-looking middle-aged woman was inside the small office opposite, dressed in a blue smock, vaguely reminiscent of Mrs. Webber. She looked hot and tired. No one else was about.

Mannering lifted the receiver, and put in his call to the *Record* and made it personal to Chittering, gave his name as Gibson. The girl at the exchange said :

" Hold on a minute, please, I'll find out if there's a delay."

Mannering waited, fiddling with the strap of the second-hand watch. A delay in calls to London might make him miss Chittering. He took out the big watch, smoothed the glass with his thumb, and the second hand ticked away, it was three minutes since the girl had asked him to wait. He forced himself to be patient, not to call the exchange again.

Then she spoke.

" Have you the money ready, sir ? "

" All ready."

" It will be three and fourpence. Will you insert the coins, please ? "

So there was no delay, and Chittering was in or the personal call wouldn't have been accepted. Coins chinked into the box. A girl said : " Just a moment, please," and then spoke to someone else : " Is that Mr. Chittering ? "

" Yes."

" You're through, Mr. Gibson," said the girl.

" Hallo, who's that ? " Chittering sounded close to the mouthpiece ; he might even have an idea who it was.

" Mr. *Gibson*," said Mannering, looking at the woman in the office. " You remember me, Chitty." He wished he could speak in his normal voice but had to keep up the accent ; the woman might hear, people downstairs might hear and notice the change. " You saw Lorna this morning, didn't you ? "

There was a pause. Then :

" You damned fool ! " said Chittering softly. " The office is crowded, the switchboard——"

" I hadn't another chance to call you. You know where the call's from, don't you ? "

" Cornwall, yes."

"There were three addresses," Mannering said. He kept his voice low, and the woman seemed to be paying him no attention. "You and everyone—got that, *everyone* including those over at Whitehall——"

"I know what you mean."

"They know the London address and the one at Guildford, do they know the one down here? If you're certain, it would be a help."

"Haven't heard it mentioned," said Chittering, "but B's a cunning cockerel when he's in the mood and the place in Devon's made them for the south-west. I saw him two hours ago. He's got round to wondering if I'd be crazy enough to lend you a helping hand. I swore that I wouldn't, but you know Bill. I'm not likely to get much more myself but I'll pick up what I can. Can I ring you back?"

"Not from the office."

"Go teach your grandmother."

Mannering found himself grinning.

"Sorry. The number is Polgissy 91. Before you ring off——"

There were noises on the telephone and then a girl's crisp voice.

"I'm sorry, caller, your time is up. If you would like another three minutes please insert——"

"Chitty," Mannering said quickly. "Check if Farley—Daniel Farley—has been in touch with B, will you? I'll be here until nine o'clock."

"Okay old boy!"

"I'm sorry, caller, but——"

"We've finished, thanks," Mannering said, and his voice sounded more north country than ever. Chittering would have reversed the charges, but it might have led to complications; Mannering's only regret was that he'd had no time to ask Chittering to trace Korra Melano. But Larraby would lose little time; and Wynne might know everything.

Mannering rang off, and went slowly downstairs. The woman still seemed uninterested in him. She wouldn't

have been able to make much of his end of the conversation even if she'd heard every word, but he wasn't at
ease; would he ever be at ease? That girl who had
interrupted—had she been listening in? Village operators
often had time to spare and listened without malice. She
might have been too busy, just chipped in when she'd a
moment to spare; if she had listened she might have
realised that the conversation was peculiar. But it hadn't
given her or anyone else anything to go on—had it?

The dining-room was reached through the bar, which
was crowded. Two men who had been there earlier
nodded to him. In the small, oak-beamed dining-room,
with room for sixteen to sit in comfort, a little old man
and a little old woman moved about quietly, helpfully,
and gave a service which was as personal and pleasing as
it would have been when smugglers or Preventive
men and perhaps the two together had sat here at a huge
rib of beef, a side of lamb or else a suckling pig. The little
old man whispered that a Spanish red wine was right,
just right, with the veal he had to serve; and it was.

A couple came in as Mannering was eating some Dorset
blue cheese and biscuits and drinking a good port, the
man with a newspaper tucked under his arm. As the
little old man whispered the youth opened the paper and
the girl read over his shoulder.

" He's ever so nice-looking, isn't he? "

" Is he? "

" You wouldn't think he was a murderer, would you? "

" Wouldn't you? "

" She looks lovely, doesn't she? "

" Sure, she's okay," said the young man, with more
interest. " Probably no better than she ought to be,
or not as good. I'll bet *they* got up to something."

" Will, *don't.*"

Mannering saw his own photograph and it didn't spoil
the port. He saw Judy's; and he had no liking left
for Dorset blue or the port. The serene quiet of the
little dining-room was broken as if by raucous cries.
He sat it out for ten minutes, was almost curtseyed to

by the little old woman and told in a whisper that the
little old man looked forward to seeing him at breakfast. Mannering smiled and said: "I'll be wi' you
all right," in his broadest north country, went out and
upstairs, to a small parlour near the telephone. When
it started to ring, he got to his feet. The fat old woman
and another whom he didn't know were in the office.

" It's probably for me."

" Is it, Mr. Gibson ? "

A voice downstairs was very clear and unmistakable;
the constable with the Christian name of Silas. He
was wishing someone good night; was he going or
coming ? Coming, probably, he hadn't been in the bar
when Mannering had crossed it from the dining-room.
Another man stopped him downstairs and they started
to talk as Mannering said :

" Hallo ? "

" A personal call for Mr. *Gibson*, please."

" It's Mr. Gibson, speaking."

" Will you take the call, please, it's from London."

" Yes, I'll take it." Why the hell need she waste
time with formalities ? Why was the policeman still
talking downstairs ? The line cackled and crackled, the
talking stopped. Mannering didn't hear a door open or
close and didn't hear footsteps on the stone steps; but
Silas might be at the foot, listening.

" You're through to Polgissy 91."

" Mr. Gibson ? " Chittering asked.

" Aye, I'm Gibson." Mannering kept his voice low
but anyone in the hall here or in the hall below would
be able to hear him. " What's ado now, man ? "

" What's ado is right," Chittering said, and the distance
didn't keep the excitement out of his voice. Was it
more than excitement—did it mean that the police were
on to the village ? " But first things first. I haven't
been able to find out if they've been in touch with Daniel
Farley or he with them, but I haven't heard of a visit
from one to the other, and they probably wouldn't leave
this to the telephone. Don't take it for granted, though."

" Not a chance." Mannering knew that Chittering was excited about something else. " And then ? "

" Listen," said Chittering ; and his voice was different, this was a warning. " A chemist's shop in Guildford was broken into last night. The burglar left no trace. A few drugs were stolen, including the kind of stuff that was used on a certain lady. Get that, Mr. Gibson— someone in Guildford last night stole the stuff."

Mannering said : " I'm getting it." The noose was drawing tighter ; it was almost as if someone had put a finger on him from the beginning and meant to keep it there. " Is that all ? "

" Not quite all. Something's just broken, very much off the record, about the other B. Remember the other B ? "

" Go on," Mannering said very softly.

" He wasn't what he seemed. Posed as a benevolent bloke with a list of charities as long as your arm. He was a fence. Know what a fence is, Mr. Gibson ? He must have been a big one. He operated on the Continent years ago, never in England, he just came here to retire. He was wanted for murder on three counts, too—killed three policemen when he escaped a cordon in Milan some time back. The photograph in the *Record* rang a bell with a man from Milan who's at the Yard now. So that's put the cat among the pigeons. I hate to say it but you've never been in a tighter spot, Mr. Gibson."

" I'm beginning to believe it," Mannering said. " Ever heard of a man named Melano ? Korra Melano ? "

" Not to remember. I'll dig deep."

" Thanks. Anything more ? " asked Mannering.

" Do you *like* punishment ? No, that's all. You'd better be good, I'm staking my reputation on you—not only with this but a splash article in the morning. Lorna sends her love."

" Give her mine," said Mannering quietly. " Give her mine."

CHAPTER XX

THE ROOF

MANNERING rang off, was conscious of the curious gaze of the younger woman in the office, turned towards the stairs to his room, appeared to change his mind and went down the stone steps. No one was in the hall. He hesitated at the door of the public bar, then thrust it open and went in. The bright-eyed policeman was playing darts with three men, all of them twenty years his senior ; he looked as if crime didn't trouble Polgissy. There wouldn't be more than two policemen in the village, and neither would be off duty if it were seriously suspected that Mannering were in the district.

Mannering bought some cigarettes and went out for a stroll. He passed five different places from which Wynne's place could be watched—three windows and two narrow alleys leading to the backs of the small shops. No one stood about. If Bristow were on to Polgissy, then Wynne's shop would be watched. Mannering stood some distance off and watched the three windows, two lighted, one in darkness. He was sure that no one was at any of them—why didn't he accept the evidence of the policeman's light-heartedness ?

It was nearly ten when Mannering reached the *Crossways Inn* again. The babble from the bar suggested that every corner was crowded and half Polgissy's residents were having a pint. Mannering didn't go in. The office and the little parlour were in darkness. He creaked his way up the stairs but didn't go to his own room. He went along a narrow passage to the bathroom, went in and locked the door, then climbed on a stool to the loft hatch. He soon had it up, and climbed into the loft.

There was a light switch.

Furniture, the usual oddments and some packing cases half-filled the boarded loft, which was surprisingly clean. Curtains hung at a window in the roof, big enough to climb through ; there was one like it in the roof at Wynne's. A coil of rope hung on a nail, used for hauling beer barrels—new rope, and just right for what he planned to do."

Mannering went back to his room, unlocked the old-fashioned door and hesitated before going in ; there wasn't the slightest reason for expecting trouble here ; and even less for being careless. He listened for a moment and heard nothing ; he would have heard breathing had anyone been there. He thrust the door open wide ; there was no movement. He put on the light and the only shadows came from chairs and a table.

He went in and closed and locked the door.

An old winged armchair was comfortable, so he had bodily comfort. He started to think again—going over everything that had tugged at his mind since Chittering's call. The burgled chemist's shop and the stolen drugs pointed a finger at him so starkly that if Bristow had ever any doubts, he wouldn't have them much longer. Mannering forgot Bristow and concentrated on the basic problem of why this was happening to him ; he didn't get far.

Farley had sent him to Blane ; Judy had called him back to the house ; and from the moment he had left in his shirt sleeves, someone had been after him, pressing that damning finger tightly. No one could have been framed more thoroughly or more cleverly.

Why ?

He'd asked the same question about the girl, wondered if there could be personal malice behind it. He could see no reason, knew none of the people concerned, had no reason to think that they knew him—yet they had known him. The two men who had seen the girl and pulled her round had made her name him. They were interested in jewels ; anyone really interested in jewels might recognise Mannering on sight. Had it been as simple as that ? Had they recognised him, seen a perfect victim, and worked up from there ?

The answer didn't satisfy him and he couldn't think of another.

He had plenty to think about besides that—perhaps the biggest thing yet, the news about William Blane. Chittering hadn't been wrong, that kind of story didn't reach the Press unless it were established beyond any doubt. So Blane, acting the part of a philanthropist, winning the fierce loyalty of Judy Darrow, had been a fence and a killer.

And someone had killed him.

The room was cold, in spite of the electric fire; and Mannering was cold because fear was at his elbow.

Bristow knew that the Baron had operated on the Continent—and now Bristow knew Blane for a continental buyer of stolen goods. He would start digging into the past. He might have doubted whether Mannering had killed Blane for the Korra emeralds; he might believe—why shouldn't he believe ?—that Mannering had killed a murderer who could give the Baron's past away.

Blane's past could give Mannering a stronger motive, the strongest possible motive, for wanting to kill him. But it wasn't Blane now, it was the girl who mattered, her death would catch the imagination of the people up and down the land, the hue and cry would become so fierce that it was hard to guess where it would end. As Mannering was now he could mix with people and get away with it—for a while. It couldn't last for long.

He had known that from the beginning.

Now he was sitting opposite Aristotle Wynne's shop. In the shop there might be an answer. It was a gamble, as much a gamble as going to the Manor. It had to be taken. He didn't want to think beyond that, because he couldn't see what to do beyond it—except work on David Graham.

Bristow wasn't a fool, Bristow would see the connection

between a doctor and a poisoned girl-friend. He would also see a connection between a burgled chemist and the Baron in the same district.

Mannering lit a cigarette, got up and put the light out, went to the window and then drew up the chair. He could watch the lighted street—there was a street lamp outside Wynne's shop, almost in front of the front door. There were lights in the big bay window, too—Wynne was probably looking down into the street. The curtains weren't drawn, but Mannering could see no one in the room, only one end of the red plush window seat.

People strolled out of the inn, went in all directions, calling good night, laughing, one man singing. Gradually silence fell. Mannering smoked three cigarettes, and during the last, heard only two couples walking past the corner ; Polgissy folk would go to bed early, but the cinema was probably not closed yet.

It wasn't. More footsteps, talk, laughter, crowds of people ebbed and flowed until they, too, fell silent as they went behind closed doors. The light still burned at Aristotle Wynne's window, and at some others—and the street lamps shone. Then the lamps began to go out, one by one. The lighted windows were darkened. One near Mannering's went out, the only light he could see now was at Wynne's window.

A car came along the narrow street from the bridge and the country beyond, slowed down, its headlights full on the big shop windows, on the oak beams, on the mass of oddments in Wynne's shop. It almost stopped outside the shop, then went on, the engine faded into the rest of the silence. Mannering waited still ; it wasn't yet twelve, he could not start until twelve—on a job which might give him everything he needed but might leave him exactly where he was.

He would make Wynne talk ; that shouldn't be difficult.

He saw a red glow of light down below, some distance from Wynne's window. The light moved—and suddenly curved a downwards arc and joined the general blackness. Mannering moved closer to the window, puzzled; someone had tossed a cigarette away, that was normal enough; but he had heard no footsteps and until then he had heard every sound from the street.

Thanks to the light from Wynne's sitting-room, he could make out the figures of two men. They didn't come to the corner but turned up a narrow alley which led to the back of Wynne's shop and to the hilly streets behind it. Mannering still heard no sound.

That worried him.

If the police were taking up their stations, ready for a night's vigil, they might move stealthily and wear rubber-soled shoes. If the police were watching it would make his task as nearly impossible as one could be; but it had to be done. He found himself standing close to the window, watching, no longer smoking; as close as this, a light would be seen in the street.

The light in Wynne's sitting-room went out.

The darkness seemed absolute for several minutes; then Mannering began to see vague shapes, the uneven outline of the roofs in the street to his left, against the grey sky. There were no stars, the moon was behind thick clouds. He stayed exactly where he was for ten minutes, then went to the door and down the stairs, with as little sound as Larraby had made, to the front door.

It was locked and bolted.

He turned towards the passages leading to the back; darkness and silence met him. He used the pencil torch, found the doors until he reached the back door, also locked and bolted. The key groaned as he turned it but the bolts moved without a sound. He stepped into the yard, turned left and left again, brushing his shoulder against a white painted wall, then reached the street.

He heard nothing, saw no one.

He waited, in a position where a policeman might wait if watching Wynne's, and the cold bit into him, but he didn't move. He couldn't say why he was worried about the two men, except that possibly they were police on the prowl. It was conceivable that the Yard had contacted the Cornish police, who had sent plain clothes men and not informed the village police.

He heard a sound, so faint that at first he wasn't sure that he was right. It came again—a soft footfall, the kind of sound that a man wearing rubber soles would make if he walked stealthily. Then a louder sound came, the clicking of a lighter. It flared. For a split second Mannering saw a face, too vaguely for him to see it clearly. The light went out, a cigarette glowed ; but Mannering had seen two men, not one.

Were they patrolling ?

They reached the street and he could just make them out. Neither spoke—or if they spoke, it was in such muted voices that Mannering couldn't hear. They turned right, away from the corner.

The police wouldn't make such a brief visit as that, if they were watching.

Mannering stayed for a few minutes longer, then turned back towards the inn. He heard a car engine, some way off but loud in the silence. It grew louder. Headlights made a ghostly glare as the car reached the crossroads and turned right, towards the bridge and the open country. Mannering couldn't be sure whether it was the car which had arrived an hour ago. It might be ; and he was sure, now, that no one was watching the shop across the road.

He went back, left the back door unlocked for possible use later, and back in his room, stood in front of the fire for ten minutes, beating his arms across his chest, getting warm again ; he would be cold enough on the roof.

It was nearly one when he left, wearing the skin tight gloves.

His pencil torch gave him light enough, the fact that no one else was on this floor meant that sounds in the loft weren't likely to be heard. He reached it by the hatch, went straight to the window in the roof. He hauled himself up. The window was close to the wide ledge outside, there was plenty of room to walk. He crouched down, thankful that there was little wind.

He knew that no one was about—was he a fool, to try to get from one roof to the other? From below, the gap had seemed only an arm's length; it was six feet or more up here. But Aristotle Wynne's roof was below him, and on it there was a ledge as wide as this and a chimney stack close by. Mannering took out the rope, uncoiled it, whirled the noose once he had sighted the chimney stack well, and hurled it. It didn't fall clean. He heard it brush against the roof and the ledge. He tried again with the same result; twice more—and at the fifth attempt, the rope held.

He coiled his end about his waist, leaving about ten feet of slack; if he jumped, missed and fell, he wouldn't fall far. He could see now as clearly as he could ever hope to see; the ledge for which he would jump showed pale against the rest of the roof.

He could take three steps, before jumping.

He backed along the ledge, tensed himself, went forward, gritting his teeth, and leapt. He was in the air for a split second but it seemed agelong before his feet touched the ledge. He was leaning forward. His right foot was on squarely, his left on the edge. He felt himself go backwards, left heel in the air. He threw himself forward again, hands outstretched, touched the chimney stack, bent his elbows and came to rest against the chimney; he was safely on the roof.

He rested for a few minutes, and during them he placed Wynne's roof window, easy to get at, although he had to walk ten yards along the ledge. He started, crouching—and then stopped.

Footsteps suddenly broke the silence.

He stood quite still, bent almost double. A man walked briskly from one of the streets towards the corner, turned it, and went past. Could he have seen that crouching figure had he glanced up?

It didn't matter.

Mannering started off again, and reached the spot from which he could reach the window. By lying on the sloping tiles he could touch the bottom ledge with his hands. He went slowly, hands stretched high, clutched the ledge of the window, felt along it for a catch—and found none. He had to get nearer, might have to use a tool, the risk of breaking glass was too great. He began to haul himself higher, and his feet left the stone ledge. He clutched the top of the window with his left hand, his chest against the glass. He twisted and turned until he was in a position to shine his torch on to the window so as to locate the catch, and actually had his torch in his hand when a light went on at the inn. The light shone on roof and window and on him.

CHAPTER XXI

THE STRONG-ROOM

MANNERING didn't move. He could see the lighted window by twisting his neck round, and that brought back pain which he had almost forgotten. He gritted his teeth as he stared at the light which bathed him and the roof, the chimney stack and the ledge. He could see a woman moving about, hair in tight curlers, what looked like a blanket round her shoulders. He was less than twelve feet away from her, and the light shone on to her big face and double chin—it was the chambermaid.

She moved across the room. He saw her open a door and go out, leaving the light on.

The danger would come, if it came at all, when she returned—but would she be able to see out of the window into the darkness ? If he kept still, it would be all right ; but his heart was thumping. The strain of keeping flat against the window, grippng the top ledge with his hand and with a knee against the bottom ledge, was almost more than he could stand. The corner of the ledge pressed against his knee, and he wanted to move it, but if he moved he might slip and make a clattering noise on the slates.

The light blazed out and there was no movement anywhere. Why didn't she come back ? Why the hell didn't she come back ?

She came, and walked straight towards the window, seemed to be looking right at him. She had to come towards the window in order to get into bed—the bed was against the wall. Why didn't she turn away ?

She was coming close up to the window.

Mannering lay there, knee pressing against the corner of the ledge with agonising pain, head twisted round, and saw the big fat face coming nearer ; as she passed the bedside lamp part of her face fell into shadow. She reached the window and stretched up her arms—*praying ?* It couldn't be, this wasn't real, this was nightmare.

She moved her arms towards each other ; she was drawing the curtains.

They didn't blot out the light completely, and there was a crack down the middle, but they blotted out the woman. Mannering moved his leg slowly, straightened it, hung at full length while the pain eased out. Then he began again, until he was lying, knees bent and body thrust forward, one shoulder against the glass. He took out his torch, shone it on the window and saw the catch —was it a catch or bolt ? He pressed closer, to see. A bolt might be much more difficult—it would be quicker to break a window ; he would have to use gummed paper to deaden the sound.

It was a simple catch. He had the right tool, with a long thin blade like a screwdriver, took it from the kit and thrust it between the window frame and the ledge. Metal scraped on metal as he pushed to one side ; the catch went back with a sharp click.

He put the tool away carefully, held the torch between his teeth and edged to one side. The hinges were showing and the roof-window opened outwards. It was only a matter of time, now, he needn't fuss, needn't worry about the streak of light coming from the maid's window.

Ten minutes later, he climbed cautiously through the window, feet first, then lowered himself slowly while gripping the ledge with his hands ; it put more strain than he liked on to his left shoulder. He held his breath as he went down. His toes touched the floor, and a moment later he stood upright in the loft above Wynne's house.

He was breathless, and waited for several minutes, doing nothing. Then he closed the window ; it would be easy to open again if he had to come out this way ; it would have to be a grim emergency if he did. He shone the torch about. Wynne's loft wasn't spick and span, like that of the inn ; dust and cobwebs, old trunks and suitcases, broken furniture, piles of old jewel-cases all looked as if they had lain there untouched for years. The cistern gurgled like a dirge.

If the loft hatch were bolted from the inside it would give a lot of trouble. It was hinged, and opened up-wards. Mannering shone the torch round the edges and saw that it was bolted but there was room round the edges for him to insert a thin pair of calipers which he took from the tool-kit. He got a grip on the bolt with these and eased it back. It squeaked, not noisily but enough to attract the attention of anyone who was awake nearby. He didn't stop until he could see space between the end of the bolt and the side of the hatch.

He pulled the cover back, looked into a passage, swung himself over and down, and stood quite still. He heard nothing. He found the light switch and put it on. This was a narrow passage, without a window, opening on to a wider passage. He didn't know what floor Wynne slept on ; there was this, two below and then the shop floor ; the ceilings were much lower. He put the light out and went ahead, using his torch, found another light and pressed that down. Two doors led from this passage. He tried each ; neither was locked.

One was a store-room, crammed with crates, pictures, Cornish pottery on shelves which ran right round the walls. It was obviously in regular use; one crate had the lid off and packing straw was strewn about it.

If he found nothing to help in the rest of the house he could search here, but this wasn't the most likely place. He moved to the next room, which was an empty bedroom and looked as if it hadn't been used for a long time.

The wooden staircase led off to the passage.

He put off the light again, crept down the stairs pressing close to the wall, paused at the next landing, and decided to manage with the torch. As the beam went slowly round, he saw an open door. He crept towards it. There was no sound, no other light. He reached the door and listened but heard no one breathing. He stepped inside, and the door squeaked faintly as it went back.

This was a large room compared with the others, and the torchlight fell on a double bed with the head against the far wall. The bedclothes were rumpled. Mannering moved towards it, saw a velveteen smoking jacket over the back of a chair, a winged collar and cravat on an old-fashioned walnut dressing-table with wing mirrors. This was Wynne's bedroom.

Wynne had come to bed and got up again.

The obvious answer was the bathroom—but there was no light anywhere.

Mannering began to smile; if Wynne were going over his secret stock——

There was no certainty that he had a secret stock; none that he was a rogue. There was no obvious reason why he had got up and gone downstairs, either. Mannering turned away from the bed, went outside, and looked into a room opposite—a tiny bathroom. There was only one other door, and it was closed. He went towards it, thrust it open a few inches, and listened to the rhythmic sound of a man or woman breathing. He ventured further in and used the torch.

A girl, about Judy Darrow's age, lay on her side, sleeping. She had dark hair and a ruddy face; she wasn't a beauty but had the comeliness of youth. Wynne's

daughter ? A maid ? His assistant ? She slept heavily
—the early hours of the morning were dead hours to
youth. Mannering withdrew silently, closed the door
and turned the key in the lock, which was on the outside.
He paused but heard nothing, the girl hadn't been dis-
turbed.

He went down the second flight of stairs, wooden but
more solid than the others. There was no light anywhere, no sign of Wynne. The sitting-room and a dining-
room were empty but for old, probably antique furniture.
He opened three doors before he found stone steps leading
down to the shop—and still there was only darkness ahead
of him.

Where was Wynne ?

Mannering heard no sounds but those of his own
making, reached a little hallway behind the shop—he
had seen the stairs he had come down from the shop
itself. He shone the light round. Against one wall
was a small work-bench, with odds and ends of jewellery
waiting for repair—a tiny lathe, all the tools of a watch-
maker and jeweller. A strange sound forced its way
into the quiet—the ticking of half a dozen watches all
hanging on little hooks, all telling the same time within
a few minutes ; it was twenty minutes past one.

A closed door stood near the bench ; it would lead
to the cellar, the strong-room—and what ? Why was
there no light, if Wynne were down there ?

The fear which had been close to Mannering for so
long, had faded after the light had shone on him on the
roof and been gradually lost in the tension of his search,
came back. It was fear of known, inexplicable things.
Fear in which Wynne played a part—as well as two men,
the curving arc of a cigarette being tossed away, the flare
of light on a face he had seen but could never identify,
the soft sound of two men walking along the stones of
the narrow passage which led beyond here—and to the
back of the house.

Mannering turned away from the open door, went
along a passage and found the back door, which opened

on to the alley.   It wasn't locked, only closed.   He opened it and peered out.   All he could see was a glow of light which came from the maid's room at the inn.   There was no sound.

The fear was very close now.

Mannering went back to the little workshop, looked at the closed door, hesitated, then pulled at the handle; it was heavy.   He tugged and it yielded, so it wasn't locked. He had it wide open and then let it go; it swung to, slowly. He looked round for something to hold it open, hesitated, and decided that it wasn't necessary, he would only have to push from the inside, and with the door closed he could put on a light.   He stepped through to a short flight of stone steps.   There was a light switch near his hand, and the light which came on was soft but sufficient; it showed a turn in the stairs.   He went down, and the door closed softly behind him.   The stairs were spiral, and worn badly in the middle.

Only silence greeted Mannering.

He turned the last twist in the stairs.   Another door, ajar, was in front of him.   It was heavy, there was a big lock, with a key in it.

Light shone from the doorway.

Fear was like a living thing at Mannering's shoulder.

He went forward and pulled the door wide open. He saw what he had dreaded to see since the fear had first caught hold of him.

Wynne lay on the floor, in a dressing-gown, with a piece of cord tight round his neck, drawn so tightly and buried so deep in the scraggy flesh that his head lolled forward like that of a dead chicken.

*   *   *

Mannering stood up from the old man, sure that he was dead; his pulse was stilled, artificial respiration wouldn't help.   The two men had done this, of course.   They had been gone for more than an hour, Wynne had probably died before they had left.   He wore slippers;   one was nearly off and showed a shiny heel. He was lying on his side, mouth slack ; and his eyes looked as if they were open.

Mannering seemed to see two other people—the fat Blane in his chair, the lovely Judy crumpled up on the floor.

He forced the picture aside, and looked round. He had to search, although he must get away from here.

It would be easy to panic. If Bristow discovered that he had been in this room——

He shut that thought out.

The strong-room was small. Three safes stood against the blank walls, one at each—the door was at the fourth. All the safes were open. They were old-fashioned, easy for a modern cracksman to force, but these hadn't been forced. A bunch of keys dangled from one.

He could guess what had happened.

The men had gone to Aristotle Wynne's room, woken him, forced him out of bed at the point of a gun, made him get his keys, forced him to come down here, had him open the safe, and then twisted the cord round his neck— as they had once twisted a stocking. They were the same men ; who could doubt that ?

Mannering had seen them ; could have stopped them ; could have followed them.

He felt sick.

He moved forward and looked into the safes. They hadn't been emptied, there were some jewel-cases and in one a mass of papers. If he did what he wanted to do, he would get away now. But here was another dead man and the mystery was as much a mystery as ever, and he was on his way to the gallows unless he could solve it. The papers might give the clue that mattered ; only important papers would be kept in a safe. Hell, of course they would !

There was no time to study them here but there might be time to sort them out and take anything that might relate to Korra. He stepped over Wynne's body and took out the papers. Title deeds of property, agreements with people in or around Polgissy, shares, insurance policies—he thrust all these aside. He found an agreement between Aristotle Wynne and Jacob Korra Melano, put it in his pocket, and picked up two envelopes, both stuck down. Then he found a note-book. He put the envelopes and notebook in his pocket, with the Korra agreement.

When he was out of here he could decide what to do. If he stayed at the inn he would come under suspicion. If he took flight, the hue and cry would start for· Mr. Gibson and the police would have his description as he was now ; it would take time, too much ·time, to change it.

Changing the clothes would be even more difficult ; he'd got away with it all once, probably wouldn't again. He glanced down at Wynne. Now two of the people whom Daniel Farley had named had died, in the same way—what about the third ? Was Lady Jane Creswell in danger ?

He reached the door.

On the stone spiral staircase stood the girl whom he had locked in the room.

CHAPTER XXII

THE DOOR

THE girl had one foot half-way between two steps, had her left hand pressed against the stone wall, and held a sword in her right—a sword he had seen on the workbench, the blade gleaming.   It was raised as if she were prepared to bring it smashing down.   She was more than a girl, she was a woman, bigger than he had realised, wearing a dark green dressing-gown and green slippers.

For a split second both stood absolutely still.

The girl moved first.

She flung the sword at Mannering as if it were a spear, turned and began to run up the stairs as Mannering ducked. The blade caught his sleeve, he felt cloth tear, then the sword clattered against the wall and to the floor. It was still clattering as he leapt forward. He could hear the patter of the girl's footsteps, could imagine her terror. She had a two yards' start, and two yards could be fatal. He turned the stairs and saw her disappearing through the doorway, hair streaming behind her. She lost one slipper and it fell down towards Mannering, lodging on a step as he put his foot down. He stumbled. The girl didn't look round, but disappeared—and the door closed.

Mannering recovered his balance and leapt up, hearing a sound which might have been of a key turning, or a bolt being shot home. There was no key in the lock this side. He flung himself against the door, and it was like pushing at a brick wall. He clenched his teeth as he grabbed the handle ; it turned but the door didn't open.

He heard no other sound.

He leaned against the door, gasping as if he had been running for miles, all the strength drained out of him. He was imprisoned and there was no time to get that door down, nothing short of dynamite or gelignite would blow it down quickly. The girl would be at the telephone by now ; if the police took ten minutes to get here that was all the time he had to work in.

He couldn't get out in ten minutes.

He couldn't quieten his breathing, either, or shake off the ague which disaster brought to him. Down the spiral staircase was the body of Aristotle Wynne. Beyond the door was the girl, at the telephone.

Mannering stood away from the door, cursing himself for his weakness, trying to make himself think. There must *be* a way out—but there would only be one way into the cellar strong-room and there just wasn't a way of getting that door down in time. He'd seen the lock, knew how long it would take to force.

Think, damn you, *think !*

He had ten minutes——

He could win more.   They could turn the key in this door
and there was no way in which he could keep them out, but
he also could barricade the door below and gain time—if
time could save him.   He went downstairs slowly ; if he
rushed he would panic again, and above all things he must
keep his head.   He looked at the walls and the ceiling, and
there was no break in them, not even a ventilator.   He
entered the other room, and examined the door.   There was
a key and there were two bolts.   He went in, closed the
heavy door and shot the bolts.

The door was so heavy that it would take the police a long
time to break it down ; did that help him ?

He stepped over Wynne's body and looked about the walls;
they were of blank stone.   He looked up at the ceiling.

For the first time he saw a glimmer of hope.

In the far corner was a ventilator, an iron grille a foot or
more square.   He went towards it slowly, fingering the tools
in his waist-band.   The iron was rusty—so were the screws
which fastened it to the ceiling.   He couldn't see above it.
He didn't try to, for where there was a ventilator there must
be an inlet for air and space beyond.   He turned towards the
smallest of the three safes, and pushed against it ; it didn't
yield.   It had to yield.   He steeled himself, pulled it towards
him, then turned it from one corner to the next ; it thumped
against the stone floor, and he had to rest.   It took him five
minutes to get it beneath the ventilator.   He stood still,
listening, hearing nothing.

The police might be out ; the girl might have trouble finding them.   She would call neighbours, but every extra
minute he gained would help.

He climbed on to the safe, bending his head to clear the
ceiling.   He examined the ventilator closely, and saw that it
had been cemented round the rivets ; the cement at one had
began to crumble.   He took out a small cold chisel and a
hammer.   The cramped space made working difficult and
the hammering made too much noise, but speed was all-im-
portant.   He had to narrow his eyes against the falling chippings, shifted his position to avoid the worst of them, kept
smashing at the cold chisel and felt it go between the cement

and a corner of the grille. He kept hammering—and something cracked loudly.

One corner was free.

He turned to the next. It was tighter, and took him longer, but it came away at last.

Dust and tiny pieces of cement were in his eyes, which watered freely, and his neck ached from the strain, but there were two corners free and he had still heard nothing from the passage. He hesitated, then heard sounds which seemed to come from a long way off.

A voice called : " Open this door ! "

The door was thick and fitted tightly, the voice seemed faint and far off, but it was there.

" *Open this door !* "

They'd forgotten half of the formula—'in the name of the law '.

Mannering climbed down from the safe, wiped his eyes but could do little to ease them ; the right eye smarted. He wiped the sweat from his forehead and neck, as the call was repeated. What did they think they would get from calling out like that ?

" *Open this door—in the name of the law !* "

Mannering's lips set almost in a grin. He judged the distance between his head and the ventilator and stretched up. On tip-toe he could grip the iron bar on the side where it had been loosened. He got his hands through the wide space between the criss-cross bars, gripped, then pulled himself upwards, all his weight on the grille. Then he tugged downwards, and he felt the ventilator sag. Given half an hour on his own there would have been no trouble, but he couldn't hope for so long.

There was a thud at the door ; they were trying a battering ram. There wasn't much room outside to swing it, but the door probably wouldn't stand much of that kind of pressure. He swung again, dragging downwards, heard a groaning sound, felt a shower of plaster chippings on his face. But when he stood upright again the grille was still in position, and his hands felt as if they had been cut with a knife.

He put his weight behind the grille again—and it gave way.

He fell, and the grille struck the side of his head, then clattered on the floor.

Mannering got up, unsteadily. The side of his head felt raw. He couldn't afford to wait. He heard the thudding and the creaking of the door as the battering ram smashed against it. How long would it hold out ?

He climbed up on the safe, and shone the torch into the ventilator shaft.

It revealed another grille, leading to the street or yard—which it was didn't matter. Outside grilles were often let into grooves and not cemented. If this were cemented he wouldn't be able to push it up, there was no way of getting enough pressure against it. He gritted his teeth so tightly that his jaws ached as he put the torch away, stretched up his arms and placed the palms of his hands against the upper grille. The shaft was about a foot deep. He bent his knees, then began to press upwards. Even if it were only in grooves, it might be too heavy for the restricted pressure he could get behind his effort.

He strained his hands against it—and felt it move.

Behind him, the thudding came at longer intervals, but more heavily ; and the door creaked more noisily. Then both sounds faded as his effort brought the blood throbbing through his head, singing in his ears. His muscles seemed to crack, but the grille moved, kept moving.

He couldn't keep it up much longer.

His arms, his legs, his shoulder—especially the left shoulder—felt as if they were being slashed with red-hot knives. His teeth seemed to grind themselves into one another—but the grille kept moving.

One more effort—just one more.

He felt it give, and the weight eased. He relaxed, and it fell back into place ; he cursed himself for the precious, wasted moment. Now he had to summon all his strength again, and his muscles were flayed almost beyond endurance. He pushed his palms against it.

It moved more easily.

He prayed that he had pushed it out of the grooves, where dirt had made it stick, that it was free. If he had, all he

had to do was shift it to one side or the other ; the grille
itself wasn't any great weight. He moved it towards the right
because he could rely on his right arm more than on the left.

It went to one side, quite freely.

He felt the fresh air sweeping into the shaft.

He heard the banging on the door.

He groped for the side of the shaft, found the edge, and
hauled himself upwards. An hour ago it would have been
easy, now it was an ordeal ; and there wasn't much room.
His shoulders brushed against the side, and seemed to become wedged. He kicked against the top of the safe, and
wriggled upwards. Soon, his head and shoulders were above
ground.

He was in a yard, could see the walls of houses on
either side, but not the street.

He heard a car moving at high speed, and behind the wall
saw the glow of headlamps.

At last he stood on the flagged yard, the hole by his side.
He needed rest desperately but dared not take a moment ;
once they broke into the strong-room they would see what
had happened and be on his heels. He waited just long
enough to get used to the darkness and to pick out the shape
of a door leading out of the yard.

The two men had used that door.

He went towards it slowly, gradually regaining the freedom
of his muscles. His hands felt as if they had been cut in two,
but he moved his fingers gingerly, to get back the circulation.

He opened the door ; it wasn't bolted, but he had no
doubt that it had been before the two men had come. He
opened it. He knew that it led to the alley which, in one
direction, led to the road with the *Crossways Inn* immediately
behind it, and in the other towards the heights on which part
of the village was built.

The car had stopped.

Headlights still glowed, and Mannering imagined there
were several cars along there. The quiet night carried voices
from outside the shop. Mannering turned towards the left
and walked up the steep alley. Now and again he stumbled,
but he walked more freely after the first few minutes. Pins

and needles stabbed at his hands but gradually eased.

He reached a road, not wide but not an alley, and stood to try to remember where it would lead.

To the left, unless it turned unexpectedly, it would lead to the main road—another left turn there would take him to the crossroads. But when he joined that main road, a right turn would take him towards the bridge and to the motor-cycle. The only danger of being wrong was that this road might change its direction.

He turned left.

Five minutes' walking brought him to the main road, which was as straight as it was narrow. A quarter of a mile or more along he saw a blaze of light, the shadowy shapes of people, and he fancied that he could still hear the murmur of voices. He turned right, and was soon able to make out the shape of the bridge with its pale grey arches. Over the bridge, Larraby had said, he would find the motor-bike hidden in a barn, under some sacking and hay.

Would it still be there ?

Could he reach it without being seen and stopped ?

CHAPTER XXIII

DOCUMENTS

MANNERING slowed down as he turned into Meybrick Road, stopped outside Mrs. Webber's house, climbed stiffly off the motor-cycle, then wheeled it up the path. He left it outside the shed where he had once parked the Buick, and went to the front door.

Mrs. Webber wasn't likely to recognise him. He tried to decide how to greet her.

He rang the bell, and there was no answer. He waited, leaning against the wall, every muscle aching. Except for two hours in a public park in Yeovil, he hadn't rested since he had found the motor-cycle and started the long ride, first through

the dark night, then through the greyness of dawn and afterwards through the brightness and unexpected warmth of a
day full of summer's promise.

It was half past three in the afternoon.

There was no answer, and Mannering looked along the
path, without much hope of seeing Mrs. Webber. Why
should he have taken it for granted that she would be in ? She
wasn't, and it brought him up against a brick wall. Rest was
important—physical and mental rest, away from the immediate threat of the police, free of the need for watching
every moment, free from the fear which the sight of the
police brought. They shouldn't recognise him—but they
might.

The wallflowers in a bed outside a front-room window
were vivid in the sun, bright red, deep red, yellow and vari-
egated growing thickly together. The bed was surrounded
by a row of bricks.

Mannering started up. One of the bricks was loose, not
embedded in the ground like the others. He went forward
almost breathlessly, bent down, moved the brick—and saw
the front-door key.

" Bless your heart," he said aloud. " Bless your heart ! "

He let himself in, closed the door after putting the key
back ; Mrs. Webber might look under the brick when she
returned and if she saw the key she would probably think
that he was still away. What would she feel about him being
here now ?

He could face that when he had to. If Larraby hadn't
recognised him, Mrs. Webber surely wouldn't. He could
talk his way through.

He went to the kitchen ; there was no smell of stale
kitchen refuse, and the small room looked spotless. In the
larder he found a tinned ham, freshly opened, bread and
butter. He cut off chunks of bread and two slices of ham, put
some butter on a plate, then washed everything up and put it
where he had found it before carrying his lunch upstairs. He
had had a fair breakfast at a little café on the outskirts of
Yeovil, but was ravenous.

His room was just as he had left it, with his suitcase.

He ate everything he had brought up, made himself some tea—Mrs. Webber had put a tea-caddy on the bedside table —and then washed; he didn't shave. He returned to the bedroom, locked the door, kicked off his shoes and took off his coat, then put the documents he had taken from Wynne's safe on a table, pulled the table to the window and sat down in the armchair. The side light was good ; he needed less sleep than complete bodily relaxation and temporary relief from the tension of being on the run.

Ash-tray and cigarettes by his side, he picked up the agreement between Korra Melano and Aristotle Wynne. It was much the same as that between the man he had never met and Lady Jane Creswell, and didn't help. He opened one of the envelopes ; there was another set of the pictures of the Korra jewels, and a few notes written in a copper-plate hand that was probably Wynne's. Wynne had recorded the history of the three sets of jewels, but there wasn't much to record. About the time that Mrs. Darrow had told Mannering that Korra had sold the emeralds to Lady Jane, he had also sold the diamonds to Wynne.

There was another note ; dated three months ago. *Korra asked me to sell the diamonds—refused. Would like to get the whole collection.*

Judging from that, Korra had been alive three months ago. Was Korra Farley's client ? Had he tried to buy the stones himself and been refused by both Blane and Wynne ? Apparently Korra hadn't known that Lady Jane had sold the emeralds to Wynne.

A note slipped between the photographs was dated much earlier, and read : *Offered Lady Jane £17,000 for the emeralds and she refused. Mortgaged another house and raised my offer to £21,000. She accepted. Wish I could have paid her what she wanted—£30,000.*

There couldn't be much stronger evidence that Wynne had been both honest and wealthy, had wanted the jewels for their own sake, and been prepared to buy them. There was no doubt at all that Korra, having sold, wanted them back—so Korra must have recovered from the shock of his wife's death, and made money again.

Would he try to buy, with Farley's help, and at the same
time steal, using two men to kill ?

Mannering hadn't liked Farley as an individual, but it was
asking too much to believe that Farley was a rogue.   If
Korra were his client, Farley at least believed that he was
reputable.   If Korra were, then who had killed and stolen ?

Who had framed Mannering ?

He didn't try to reason why he had been framed, just
accepted the facts—but they led to one deduction that he
hadn't made before.   If the killers had selected him, Mannering, as a victim before he had gone to Blane's house for a
second time, then it meant that they had known Mannering
was after the rubies and would probably visit Blane again.

Judy had known—and might have told others.   Certainly
she might have told Graham, but he had been in the north,
she wouldn't have telephoned him.   Blane might have told
others.

Why should he ?

There was a thin note-book, every page filled with copper-
plate writing—like the price tickets in Wynne's shop window.
Mannering began to read, quickly at first, then more slowly.

The paper was old, the ink black with age, but the story
was as fresh and clearly told as one could be.   Here was the
story, written as extracts from a diary, of the long association
between Jacob Korra Melano, Lady Jane, Wynne and—at a
later stage, ten years after they had first worked together—
William Blane.

It was clear that Korra had been the leading light.   Big
deals in jewels, *objets d'art* and money had been put through.
Korra had used the others as a front while making vast
profits—and then, after his wife's death, Blane had tricked,
cheated and ruined him.   To get out of his difficulties,
Korra had started buying and selling stolen jewels.   It hadn't
been in a big way.   Korra had been sentenced to three
years' penal servitude, at the West Country Assizes.

The story was told without emotion, and it stopped after
Korra's ruin.

Mannering stubbed out a cigarette, looked at a few white
clouds drifting sluggishly across the sky, shook his head

slowly and picked up the other sealed envelope.   He opened
it and shook out a number of papers, all formal-looking—
birth certificates, death certificates, marriage certificates.
Wynne's birth certificate was there, but apparently he hadn't
married.

Who was the dark-haired girl ?

Lady Jane had been born Lady Jane Gorring, had married
twice—first a William Morris, then Charles Creswell.   She
had had one son, by her first marriage.   It was the entry in
the last column of the son's certificate which made Mannering grip the paper so tightly that it was creased between his
thumb and forefinger.   Under the column headed ' *Christian
Names* ' there were two : William *Blane*.

Had Blane been Lady Jane's son ?

Gradually Mannering relaxed.

This was something so unexpected that the effect of the
shock lingered but—did it help ?   The old lady was over
eighty, frail, almost blind according to Stella Darrow.   A
shock might kill her.   But she had been a close associate
of Korra.   She might know much more than Stella Darrow
had professed to know.

Was there a way of making Lady Jane talk ?

Apart from finding David Graham and working on him,
there was no other angle.   The two men were just vague
figments on his mind—shadowy, unnamed, unknown.
Only dead Judy had seen them.

Graham, knowing the extent of Mannering's danger,
wouldn't be easy to frighten into talking, for he had his own
neck to save.   *Could* there be any doubt that Graham had
killed Judy ?   Obviously someone else *could* have put the
morphia tablets into that Aspirin bottle, but the odds that
it had been Graham seemed short.   Graham appeared to be
Mannering's one chance.   Should he take it before or after
trying to learn what Lady Jane knew ?

He said aloud : " After, I fancy," and then stopped
thinking, for footsteps sounded on the stairs.   He had heard
Mrs. Webber come up often enough to know hers, and someone else was with her.

Man or woman ?

Had the newspaper stories been too much for Mrs. Webber? Had she told the police and brought them to search the room? There was only one person with her as far as he could judge—Bristow wouldn't come alone.

He stood up, slowly.

The handle of the door rattled, and then Mrs. Webber said loudly: " Why, it's locked."

" Then he's back ! " another woman said.

Lorna had come with Mrs. Webber.

*　*　*

At first all Mannering thought about and cared about was that Lorna stood outside. The fact that she would almost certainly have been followed by the police came later.

*　*　*

" But the key was under the brick," protested Mrs. Webber. " You saw it with your own eyes, didn't you ? "

" Yes, but the door *is* locked, isn't it ? " Lorna's voice was steady but higher pitched than usual, with excitement she was trying to keep back. The handle rattled again.

Mannering said : " Just a minute."

He heard Mrs. Webber exclaim. Lorna said nothing. He went slowly to the door. He would soon know whether Mrs. Webber was still prepared to play. He couldn't keep his mind off that. If ever he had wanted to greet Lorna on her own, this was the moment, yet Mrs. Webber could make or break him.

He unlocked the door.

Mrs. Webber stood in front, her big body keeping Lorna from the room. Mannering looked over her shoulder and into Lorna's eyes, saw the blaze of relief and excitement, knew that for her his voice had stripped the disguise away. It hadn't for Mrs. Webber. She backed a pace, looking scared. Lorna moved out of her path. Mrs. Webber, massive as a battleship, recovered from the surprise and raked Mannering with her bright blue eyes and said :

" Who the devil are *you* ? "

" Mannering sent me," Mannering said, and became north-country Gibson again. " He told me where to find the key and——"

" Oh, did he," said Mrs. Webber. " It's one thing letting a boarder come in, quite another letting any Tom, Dick or Harry walk into a lady's house when she's out. Is he coming back ? "

" That depends on whether you——"

" I've just told Mrs. Mannering that if he comes back he can stay until dark and then he'll have to go. I can't help what Josh Larraby says, I can't help what *any*one says. I'm beginning to wonder if Mannering did kill that girl. That was a *wicked* thing. I can't take any more chances, but I'll keep my word—so long as the police don't come here. If they ask questions I'll tell them what I told Mannering himself I would. See ? " Mrs. Webber was less truculent than definite. " How long are *you* going to stay ? " she asked Lorna.

" Not long," Lorna said quietly.

" If you want a cup of tea, he can make it for you," Mrs. Webber said. " I'm not climbing those stairs again with tea for anybody."

*   *   *

' So long as the police don't come here,' Mrs. Webber had said, and the momentary relief from fear vanished. Bristow would never let Lorna escape his men, would be sure that sooner or later she would go to Mannering. The shadow was there as he pulled Lorna in, closed the door, and gripped her hands. Then his arms went round her and her cheek was pressed against his. She made little sobbing sounds, as if she had not dared to hope.

He could hear her heart pounding through the softness of her breast.

They stood like that for a long time, and before she moved away, Mannering was thinking that the police might be turning into the gateway.

Lorna stood back ; there were tears in her eyes but she was

trying to smile. She walked away from him and wiped her eyes with her fingers, turned with her back to the window, and said unsteadily :

" Not hurt ? '

" I'm fine."

" It's all right," Lorna said. " No one followed me, darling, I'm quite sure."

" How can you be ? " He hated himself for saying it, but there was hardly another thought in his mind.

" I am sure," she said. " I've been sitting in a car—I hired one—for half an hour, at the end of the road. Then I got out and walked round the block. No one followed me. I went to Harrods, and they couldn't cover all the exits. It's all right, darling."

Probably no one else could have convinced him so quickly. He felt himself relax, felt the reaction sharply and sat on the side of the bed, looking at her. She moved to him, pressed his head against her breast, then backed away quickly.

" This won't do ! I was afraid you'd never get away from Cornwall."

" Do you know what happened there ? "

" It's in the evening papers," Lorna said. " Chittering told me, before that. He also told me that Farley went to the Yard this morning."

Mannering felt for cigarettes, lit one and found himself grinning.

" Bristow won't have thanked him for being late ! Perhaps we owe Farley more than we know, if he'd gone yesterday morning——" he broke off, and Lorna took a folded sheet of newspaper from her handbag and handed it to him. It was the front page of the *Evening Cry*, Wynne's picture was there with that of the girl, the story seemed to shriek at him. His own picture was there, too, and the caption— *John Mannering, the wanted man.*

Lorna said : " I can imagine what happened. You got there and found him dead, but——" she broke off. Her beauty was clouded by the shadows in her eyes. " How are you going to convince anyone ? Blane—Judy Darrow—Wynne. Who's doing it, John ? Who means to get you hanged ? Why——"

" Easy," Mannering said. " The who matters, the why will come after it. David Graham's got a few questions to answer and there's another line, in——"

" But you can't go on like this," Lorna said tensely. " You look—oh, you look as if you could fall asleep on your feet. You can't have slept for two nights. There isn't a policeman in the country who isn't looking out for you. It won't last, John, you can't stand the pressure. I'm beginning to believe that Farley was right, you ought to give yourself up. Bristow's fuming now but when he calms down he'll see reason, he'll follow up everything you tell him, and——"

" We haven't just Bristow to deal with," Mannering said. " It's the Commissioner at the Yard, the Public Prosecutor, all the Queen's men ! " He spoke quite mildly. " We need a lot more than we've got to shake them, you can be sure Graham's protected himself. But I'll tackle him after I've tackled Lady Jane Creswell. I should have made sure of her the first time. I——"

" You can kill two birds with one stone," Lorna said quickly. " Graham's at The Manor, with Judy's mother. But you'll never get there. Lady Jane is the only one of the three alive, Bristow will surround The Manor while there's a ghost of a chance of you turning up. I hate to say it but I don't think there's any hope, unless——"

She didn't finish.

CHAPTER XXIV

WAY IN

POLICE stood on guard at the gates leading to The Manor. Others were at the several places where it would be easy for a man to force his way through the hedge. Cyclists patrolled the lanes and men on foot patrolled the edge of the clear ground. Cars were stationed at various points

and their headlamps showed up the trees and the grass,
made a barrier of light against which anyone who tried to
break through would be seen.

Two Yard detectives, working with the Surrey
Police, were stationed at the main entrance to the
house; and to make the possibility of a break-through
virtually impossible, two men stood at each of the other
doors.

Superintendent Bristow had been round himself, walking
where it was impossible to take a car, and had been satisfied.
Satisfied, that was, by the precautions. Those who knew
him well declared that they had never known Bristow in
a worse mood. There were those who doubted whether
Mannering would try to get in, but anyone who thought
that the precautions were unnecessary didn't say so in
Bristow's hearing; and the knowing ones said that no one
at the Yard knew Mannering so well as Bristow, or was
more likely to judge his next move. A few knew that
another house was as closely guarded—Daniel Farley's
not far away. Farley had a guest—Mr. Jacob Korra
Melano, who might be in as much danger as the other
victims.

The moon shone from a clear sky, higher and much
brighter than when Mannering had first come here.

A car came along the road from the village, its headlights blazing. Near the main gates the engine slackened,
the car almost stopped, then came on smoothly again.
Everyone in Melbury and most of the police from Guildford knew the venerable old Rolls-Royce which Dr. Jewett,
who had attended Lady Jane for the past twenty years,
loved with a great love. None of the watching men was
surprised to see the doctor's car; it had come in and out
two or three times that day, as often the day before. Dr.
Jewett was attending Lady Jane for shock and Mrs. Darrow
for much the same reason.

A constable stepped into the roadway and the car slowed
down.

" What's this ? " Jewett asked. He had a rumbling voice
and he sounded annoyed; a shrewder man than the con-

stable might have thought he sounded frightened. " What's this, eh ? "

" Sorry, doctor, but I've had orders."   A torch beam fell on to the doctor's face and on to the face of the woman, in nurse's uniform, sitting with him. " Lady Jane's not worse, is she ? "   The torch wavered, flashed over the back seat, actually touched the top of a rug which lay over Mannering who crouched in the roomy landaulette ; it soon went out. " I mean, does she need a nurse ? "

" If you've no objection," Dr. Jewett said stiffly, " she does."

" Sorry, sir, I meant no offence."

Jewett grunted and drove on. Twenty yards from the gates the engine nearly stalled again and the old car almost stopped.   The policeman watched it, and grinned faintly.

" Touchy tonight, isn't he ? Serve him right if he has to walk up the hill."

It looked as if Dr. Jewett would have to walk, for half-way between the gates and the house, the car stopped.   The grating noise of the self-starter sounded clearly, every man on duty heard it ; most of them saw the car standing with the headlights still blazing.   The drive was over half a mile long, the men had strict orders not to leave their posts, so none went to help Dr. Jewett, although Dr. Jewett badly needed help.

* * *

" I'm sorry about this," Mannering said.   He sat forward on the edge of the back seat, with a hypodermic needle in his hand.   " Just a prick you know—and you'll only go to sleep for an hour or two.   Don't struggle, or the needle will break in your neck."

Jewett's voice had a note of bravado, but he couldn't hide the fact that he was frightened.

" You'll suffer for this. If you're the devil who killed——"

" No devil," Mannering said, and jabbed the needle.

The headlights shone out in front of the car, dimming

every time Lorna pulled the self-starter. She switched
them off. Dr. Jewett, still frightened, did exactly what he
was told. It was easy to climb over the front seat of the
big old car, and to take the place where Mannering had
been. His neck smarted a little where the needle had
plunged home. It was the second injection; the devils
had learned how to give knock-out drops, with a small
dose first, a booster for quick action soon afterwards.
Jewett was already feeling the weight of unconsciousness
closing in on him.

Mannering climbed to the seat next to Lorna.

He didn't take Jewett for granted, but turned awkwardly
and looked down at the man—and was in time to see Jewett
rise up and grab at the door handle. He squeezed the back
of the doctor's thick neck, pressed hard, and forced Jewett's
nose to the floor. Jewett resisted, but soon went limp.
Mannering put the rug over him.

"Game old boy," Mannering said, and turned round
in his seat. Lorna pulled the self-starter again and the
grating noise must have sounded all over the grounds.
Mannering, wearing a blue raincoat, put on a peaked
chauffeur's cap.

"Know the drill?" Mannering asked, and tried to
sound casual.

"I shan't forget," Lorna said. "What's going to
happen if they don't let you go in?"

"We don't even think of it," Mannering said. "One
thing at a time." The self-starter worked smoothly and
the engine started. He drove towards the house, and pulled
up right outside the entrance, very close to the steps.
The big car hid most of the porch and most of the two men
on duty there from those at the gate. Mannering opened
the door, nodded to the two men, hurried round and
opened the door for Lorna. She wore a grey cloak and a
starched white uniform and starched white cap.

"Dr. Jewett's sent a night nurse for Lady Jane," he said.
"And I've got to have a word with Mrs. Darrow."

If they challenged him, he knew exactly what he was going
to do; and knew that it would shorten the odds drastically.

They might question but wouldn't be prepared for attack. The car should hide what happened from all watchers, and he had the knock-out drops in reserve. He didn't know that Bristow had made his one mistake, stationing two Yard men at the door instead of one Yard and one local man, who would know that this wasn't Dr. Jewett's chauffeur.

Mannering had changed his make-up, hunched his shoulders and padded his coat to make himself look shorter, and his face was pale, almost pasty.

He recognised one of the Yard men, who looked at Lorna. Did the man recognise her? Lorna had made up less than usual; the nurse's cap gave her face a severe look, and she wasn't so well known as Mannering.

"How long will you be?" the man asked, and the other obligingly rang the bell. Why not? The men at the gate, who knew the local people, had let them in and sent no signal; it was good enough.

"Depends on Mrs. Darrow," Mannering said.

They stood on the porch, Mannering stiffly, the others more interested in Lorna than in the chauffeur. A butler opened the front door, the hall light fell on both chauffeur and the nurse.

"Mrs. Darrow, please," the nurse said briskly.

"And I've to wait for a message," Mannering said.

"I see," said the man who had opened the door. He was tall and ageing, with grey hair and a sad face—not really like Aristotle Wynne but reminding Mannering of the Polgissy dealer. "I'll tell her."

He closed the door.

"If you'll wait here——"

"Mrs. Darrow's expecting us," Lorna said. "Is she upstairs, or——"

"She's in her room, miss. I don't know that——"

"Well, take us up if you want to." Lorna was sharp, almost shrewish. "She telephoned——"

"I think I'd better take you," the man said. He led the way up the wide staircase, puzzled but not suspicious. He went straight to the door of the room where Mannering

had found Mrs. Darrow and mistaken her for Lady Jane.
There was a light at the sides and at the bottom. He tapped,
and Mrs. Darrow called :

" Come in."

The butler opened the door.

" It's the nurse, ma'am, and Dr. Jewett's chauffeur,
apparently, he——"

Lorna pushed past him. He saw Mannering's hand move
and hardly knew what had struck him—there was just a
sharp pain at his chin and his teeth clicked together and
something seemed to burst in his head.

He didn't know that Mannering saved him from falling,
or that Lorna, a gun in her hand, covered Mrs. Darrow,
who sat by the fireplace, firelight on her dressing-
gown, her hair and her eyes, a photograph album on her
lap.

Mrs. Darrow leaned forward, caught her breath, and her
mouth was open as she stared. Mannering closed the door
behind him softly, lifted the butler and carried him across
the room. The woman watched him, then looked back
at the gun. Mannering took two lengths of cord from
his pocket, bound the man's wrists and ankles, stuffed a
piece of cloth into his mouth, and bundled him under the
bed.

Mannering stood up.

" Hallo, Stella," he said.

Stella Darrow recognised him then. Her mouth closed
slowly and she started to get up. The album fell from
her lap. She stood upright, and Lorna took a step towards
her. She ignored the gun.

She said : " You—*you've* the damnable nerve to come
back *here*. After——" her eyes blazed, she moved
swiftly towards Mannering, behaved as if there were no
nurse, no gun. "My God, I'll strangle you with my own
hands!"

She flung herself forward. Mannering dodged, caught
her right wrist and twisted sharply ; the pain stopped her.
He held her arm up, and remembered when they had
struggled for the gun, and stood as close together as this.

He said : " Do you want to find Judy's murderer ? "

" You—you killed her, you——"

" Wrong," he said.   " I was just the stooge who happened along.   Fond of your daughter ? "   If she were this would hurt, and it did hurt ; he could see that in her eyes, mixed with hatred for him—and perhaps a gleam of doubt.

" So you were," he said.   " Fond of David ? "

" Let me go, or I'll shout, I'll——"

" I asked if you were fond of David," Mannering said roughly.   " If you are, you'll change.   He gave Judy her handbag, she'd left it at his flat.   He changed aspirin tablets for the drug that killed her.   Dear David !   Why should he want to kill her ?   Do you know ? "

The doubt was there now, he didn't question that ; the woman fought against it.

" If you think you can make me believe that David——"

" I'm here to prove it.   Where is he ? "

" Downstairs, I expect, he——" she broke off.   " It can't have been *David*."

" Why not ? "

" She loved him so much," Judy's mother said, and her eyes closed as if to shut out a nightmare picture.   " When I went to see her at the nursing home, she wanted David, it was all David.   I was glad Blane was dead."   She opened her eyes wide, passion stormed in them.   " I was glad, do you hear ?   He had taken possession of Judy, I sometimes wondered if he'd warped her soul.   She was fiercely loyal, admired him so, was torn between loyalty and love for David—no, I don't believe it !   I just don't believe it could have been David."

" Why is he still here ? "

" I—I don't know.   Do you need a reason?   He's grief-stricken, heart-broken.   Lady Jane doesn't mind whom I have to stay.   She thinks he's company for Bill, too."

There wasn't much time, and the minutes were flying, but there had to be time to talk about this.

" Who's Bill ? "   Mannering asked.

Stella Darrow looked as if that didn't matter, and couldn't

bring her mind to answering questions. The look of
defiance mingling with disbelief was in her eyes.

"Her son. He's just come home from abroad. He
doesn't often visit her. He——"

Mannering said softly : "So her son's come home." The
truth began to dawn on him then, but he wasn't sure ; it
was a flash of revelation which wouldn't help unless he
could soon prove it true. Lorna saw the change in his
expression, even Stella Darrow was affected.

"So her son's come home," Mannering repeated.
"William Blane Morris. Where is he ? "

"In his room. What—*what* did you say ? "

"I just told you his full name," Mannering said.
"Where's his room ? "

She was almost incoherent.

"Along—along the narrow passage. But——"

"Which door ? " As if he couldn't find the room.

"The second," she said. "What are you going to do ?
What——" she opened her mouth, as if to scream.

Mannering said : "Watch her, my darling." He
hesitated, swung round, snatched a handkerchief from his
pocket. He drew the woman nearer and as she opened her
mouth wider, he thrust the handkerchief in ; a choking sound
came instead of a scream. He bound her wrists and took
the gun from Lorna. "No one will hurt you," he said, and
swung towards the door.

No one was in the passage.

Light edged the door of the room where Lady Jane's son
was supposed to be.

CHAPTER XXV

MAN ALIVE

MANNERING turned the handle slowly, and pushed. The
door was locked. He could hear men talking—was David

Graham here as well as the son ?   He knelt down and shone
his torch into the keyhole ; the key was in the other side.
He took out a tool with a cylindrical end, adjusted it,
pushed it into the keyhole slowly, felt it go stiffly between
the key and the lock, pushed it a little further and then
began to turn it.

Unless the men inside looked at the door, Mannering
would have it open before they had warning.   Danger
would come at the last moment, when the key would
click home.   He twisted it with almost agonising slowness,
then heard it click.   Had the men inside heard ?

Mannering stood upright, listening tensely; the murmur
of a man's voice went on and on.

He opened the door a crack ; then a few inches.

A young man, David Graham, sat at an angle from which,
if he glanced round, he could see the door.   Another sat
in a high-backed wing chair with his back towards the door.
He was talking.   Although there were no breathless pauses,
the voice was familiar ; and if Mannering wanted further
proof, he had it when the man laughed.

" Tee-hee-hee."   William Blane sounded highly amused.
" I keep telling you, David, you worry too much.   The
police aren't interested about who's *in*side here, they're
only making sure Mannering doesn't get in.   He won't—he
can't, it's impossible.   No one will recognise me from that
old photograph.   The police know the son of the house has
come home.   All I have to do is stay in my room until they
call their watchdogs off.   They'll do that as soon as they've
caught Mannering.   Tee-hee-hee."

" Very funny," said Mannering, and went in.

Graham reared up in his chair ; Blane turned his fat
neck.   Both stared at Mannering and into the muzzle of a
gun.   They sat as if petrified.   Mannering closed the door
but didn't lock it, moved towards them until he was only a
few yards away from each.

" Remember me, Mr. Blane ? " he asked softly.

Blane was pale from make-up as well as fear.   He had had
his hair cut so short that his head was almost shaved.   He
had bleached his hair, his eyebrows and his lashes.   He

wouldn't be easy to recognise at a glance, but he was recognisable—he could have learned a thing or two about make-up. His fat hands lay on the arms of his chair, quite steady—he looked like a block of ice chipped into human shape.

Graham's hands weren't steady, nor were his lips.

" W-w-who——"

" The name is Mannering," Mannering said. " We haven't met, have we, Graham ? Nice headache tablets you put into Judy's bag."

Graham tried to speak but couldn't get the words out. He half rose from his chair, then dropped back again, as if his legs wouldn't support him.

" Now I know you've got some nerve," Blane said. His voice didn't quiver. " Now I know you're good, too, but you're not soo good, Mannering. You'll never get out of this jam, not as long as you live. There's too much evidence against you, when there wasn't any you made it for yourself. Nice timing at Polgissy, and convenient of you to be with Judy when she went to sleep." His voice was a sneer. " What the hell do you think you're going to do, now you're here ? "

Mannering looked at the frightened Graham and didn't speak. Blane began to get up ; he was fat enough to have to help himself by pressing his hands against the chair arms.

" You haven't a chance," he repeated. " Any fool would see that."

Graham said hoarsely : " But if he's caught here——"

" They'll think he came after Lady J.," Blane said.

" They'll know I came after you and David," Mannering said harshly. " I shall tell them so. You may be right, and I haven't a chance. I don't like the idea of hanging for murders I didn't commit, if I'm going to hang it'll be for a couple that I did. If they'll call this murder." He still watched Graham most of the time although he kept Blane covered. He looked deadly. " You framed me too well, Blane, I just haven't a chance. But I'll make sure you two don't live to a ripe old age." He levelled the gun at Graham, was ready to swing it towards Blane—but Blane was too far away to be much danger, and wasn't likely to be able to move swiftly. "There isn't any time to spare, either, the police will be here in a minute. Just think of Judy, David. The only difference is that she didn't know she was going to die."

"Don't!" Graham gasped. "Don't——"

"Keep quiet, you fool!" Blane cried. "He won't shoot."

Mannering backed a pace, lifted his head, and began to laugh; and it wasn't a good sound to hear. It affected even Blane, who put his hands back towards his chair, as if for support. It was high-pitched, maniacal laughter, which chilled the blood and turned Graham's fear into terror.

"So I won't shoot? You think I won't shoot!" Mannering laughed again, but covered Graham's chest, then lowered the gun a shade. "The belly hurts most, Graham. Just think of Judy, just think——"

"Don't shoot!" cried Graham. "I didn't mean to kill her. He made me, it was Blane. I—I didn't know they were deadly, I thought they were headache tablets. I swear I thought they were headache tablets!"

"You killed her and I'll hang for it, so——"

"You needn't hang! I know what happened, I can save you, I can——"

Blane was watching Graham, not Mannering; and Blane hadn't put his hands behind him just for support, he was taking something out of his hip pocket. Mannering gave him just enough time to bring a gun forward, then fired. The bullet shattered Blane's wrist. Blane's gun fell, Graham began to tremble and to stare at Mannering with his mouth open, terror filling his eyes.

"So you'll clear me," Mannering said.

"I'll tell them the truth. Blane—Blane framed me, too, I didn't kill Judy. *He* tampered with the tablets."

"Keep that story up," Mannering said, "it might save your neck. Go over and pick up that telephone, tell the exchange to tell the police that Mannering's here."

*   *   *

When Graham had done that, he began to talk.

*   *   *

An hour afterwards, Mannering stood between two Yard men in Mrs. Darrow's bedroom. Bristow was on his way from London. Lorna and Mrs. Darrow were in the room, the old butler had been taken from under the bed, suffering from nothing worse than fright.

" It'll be all right," Mannering said to Lorna. " Now they know the dead man's come to life they'll see the phony side. Graham's already talked to some of the police, anyhow, and Blane will be taken from hospital to a cell as soon as his hand is dressed. It won't go wrong, my darling."

Lorna knew that it wouldn't.

Stella Darrow said huskily : " It mustn't go wrong."

*   *   *

Two weeks later, Mannering entered the sunlit office of Daniel Farley, where the mahogany desk was polished as brightly as ever and the room looked free from dust. Farley sat at his desk. A frail old man sat in another chair. This man had a wrinkled skin and a fringe of white hair, but a face which showed that once it had been strong ; a face, even now, of character.

Farley stood up quickly.

" Ah, Mr. Mannering." He stretched out his hand, seemed eager to take Mannering's. " You're most welcome. And I think you're anxious to meet my—ah—client. Mr. Jacob Korra Melano."

Korra had a surprisingly strong handclasp.

" Let me add my congratulations to the many you have had, Mr. Mannering." His voice was gentle.

Mannering moved his hands, as if pushing congratulations aside.

" Forget it. Even now I don't know all the ins and outs, I hope you're going to clear everything up, Mr. Farley."

" Oh, I think so," Farley said. " With what I know, what the police have released and with what Graham told you, I think we can piece the whole story together. It begins many years ago, of course, when Mr. Melano was at the threshold of a quite remarkable career. He numbered Wynne, Lady Jane Creswell—Morris, as she was then—and Morris, her first husband, among his friends. Her son, William Blane Morris, was then at school. Mr. Melano quite legally, conducted much of his business secretly, using the names of his friends who were, of course, well paid for their assistance. Mr. Melano's business was widespread, his influence was felt in financial circles, in fine art—but I don't think I need go into much detail about that.

" He was, of course, always *strictly* honest. He did not use his full name, in business, and was known generally as Jacob Korra.

" At the time of Mrs. Melano's death, he was so distressed that he lost immediate control of his affairs. He was glad to accept help—and most of the so-called help came from William Blane Morris, by then an able young man, in fact a young man with a very keen mind. What Mr. Melano didn't know, of course, was that Blane—we'll continue to call him that—had already been practising the gentle art of receiving stolen goods, mostly on the Continent, using Mr. Melano's Continental trade channels for this purpose. Blane then saw the opportunity of making a fortune by usurping complete control of Mr. Melano's affairs. He did so, first by pretending to act as the principal, and then by having Mr. Melano appear to be guilty of the many crimes Blane himself had committed. In fact, Blane had planned to do that for many years."

Farley paused, took a sip of water from a glass on the desk, and murmured : " Am I making it quite clear ? "

" Yes. Thanks."

" Good. Blane himself, however, did not prosper as much as he hoped after Mr. Melano went to prison. International conditions caused him great losses. He returned to his receiving on the Continent. He was almost caught in Milan where he murdered three Italian policemen in order to escape.

" He came to England, planning to spend a few years in —ah—retirement. Mr. Melano finished his sentence and went to South America, where he prospered in business.

" Mr. Melano had always intended to try to buy back his late wife's jewels. He returned to England, to try. He went to Wynne, in Cornwall, but Wynne was reluctant to sell, wanting the jewels for their own sake. By chance— bad chance for Blane—Wynne had seen and recognised him in London, and found out where he lived. Wynne told Mr. Melano, who went to see Blane, hoping—willing—to buy back some of the jewels.

" This visit coincided with a discovery that alarmed Blane. The Italian police had sent a detective to England and the Yard was helping him to trace the murderer of the three Milan police. Blane had two Italian crooks still working for him, as well as David Graham. In spite of the reputation he was building up as a philanthropist, Blane saw the red light. One of his men had been questioned. He had to get away quickly and create another identity.

" When you called on him, Mr. Mannering," the solicitor went on quietly, " he had made his plans. He was to return to his mother's home, take on his real, full name, and he hoped, live in peace. However, Judy, Wynne and Mr. Melano could betray him ; each had to die.

" He worked out an ingenious, perhaps a too ingenious plan. He arranged for a stand-in, one might say, resembling him in looks and figure, to be killed, as William Blane. The police, including the Italians, would think their hunt was over. His victims were to die *after* his own ' death '. His plans went wrong because you appeared, Mr. Mannering."

Farley paused. Mr. Korra Melano gave a slight depre-
cating smile. Farley took a sip of water, and went on :

" Blane made a number of mistakes, not all obvious when
committed. Employing Judy Darrow turned out to be
one. Using his own second name was another—but at the
time he did so he had not thought there was any risk from
Italy, as he had been known there under an *alias*. Perhaps
it was a mistake, also, to allow David Graham, a young
doctor whom he was able to blackmail since Graham
had dealt illegally in drugs, going about with Judy. Judy,
as you know, fell in love with Graham. Graham was not,
however, in love with her. In spite of all his protestations,
there is little doubt that Graham is a very vicious and evil
young man."

Farley paused again ; no one else spoke, but Korra
proffered his cigar-case to Mannering, and pierced and lit
a cigar when Mannering refused.

" The one big, the fatal mistake Blane made, however,
was to decide to kill his stand-in and to try to throw the
blame on you, once he knew you were to see Judy. He
knew about her late telephone call, of course, and made a
swift decision, thinking that while the police were hunting
you, he could make his escape and take up life at The
Manor.

" Judy was attacked first. You saved her. Before you
arrived the stand-in had been killed ; you were attacked
and Blane and his Italian accomplices returned, to ' force '
the safe. Judy was coming round. She didn't see Blane,
only the Italians and the dead man. She immediately
thought Graham, who had been blaming Blane for not
letting him marry Judy—in fact, he had no intent to marry
—was the murderer. Blane quickly turned this, as he
thought, to his advantage. His men told her what to
say in order to save David Graham. Distraught, she
obeyed.

" This hurried plan soon began to recoil. Judy wanted
to go to see her mother. Graham took her. He had made
morphia tablets to look like aspirins, which Judy took
frequently for headaches. Graham believed he could

make her death appear to be suicide. Graham had no idea you would be at the Manor House, of course.

" The Italians, meanwhile, went to Cornwall, to murder Wynne and take most of his jewels. Mr. Melano was known to be leaving the country shortly, and was regarded as a safe risk."

Farley stopped, linked his hands so that the shiny desk reflected them, his starched cuffs and gold links, and then went on slowly :

" You know what followed, Mannering. There is little doubt, I think, that Blane began by believing that Mr. Melano would be suspected of the murder of the stand-in and of the others ; the motive was there. There is no doubt that the presence in London of the Italian detective and the fact that he had already drawn close, forced Blane to act hurriedly and upon what seemed a brilliant idea to implicate you. It could have succeeded."

Mannering said dryly : " Yes. You were half-persuaded, weren't you ? "

" I was in two minds. I did not wish Mr. Melano to be involved, since he had so strong a motive—revenge for past infamy—to murder Blane. I thought Blane was dead. My intervention would have done you little good, for I would simply have given the police a reason for you going to see Blane. I played for time."

" Which Mr. Mannering used to the best possible advantage," Mr. Jacob Korra Melano said quietly. " I sit back and marvel at what you achieved."

" You'd do a lot of peculiar things with the noose as tight round your neck as it was round mine," Mannering said. " The one regret is Judy. Sure Graham knew what he was doing ? "

" I think we'll find that he did. The two Italians have been arrested, of course, on Graham's information. They probably know the truth. One of the things they did, when learning from Graham of Judy's disappearance with you, was to break into a chemist's shop in Guildford and steal some morphia. The idea was undoubtedly Graham's ;

he saw a way of escaping from suspicion and, of course, was practically certain that Judy would take those tablets while with you."

" It stands up," Mannering said. " Do you know why Aristotle Wynne kept such precise records ? "

" Oh, yes," said Farley. " After the break up of the association, he was a victim of attempted blackmail. The blackmailer tried to make out that he had worked with Mr. Melano. Wynne, a cautious man, realised that it could happen again, was prepared to believe that Mr. Melano had in fact a criminal history, and collated all the information, so that if he were ever threatened, he would have a convincing statement to offer to the police. He obtained various documents, not all relevant. It was partly due to Wynne's peculiarly orderly mind and temperament, of course."

" I am distressed, greatly distressed, for Wynne," said Korra. " And for the child, his ward, who worked with him. She was very clever at unlocking her door, Mr. Mannering, wasn't she ?   Being used to the mechanism of clocks and watches she found that fairly easy, of course. I understand she will continue with the business, so she will be all right. There is one other thing. The jewels I am so anxious to obtain will now be held at the discretion of the various executors. Those stolen from Wynne have been recovered, of course. I hope you will act as my agent to buy them for me ?   I even hope you will allow me to pay the commission in advance, five per cent on a hundred thousand pounds."

" Five thousand pounds," Farley murmured.

Mannering chuckled. " My wife will say that I've earned it," he said. " You're very good. Thanks."

*   *   *

Mannering walked away from Farley's office towards the black Rolls-Bentley, parked not far away—it had been found by the police on the day after the final affair at The Manor. He was thinking of Judy. She had told him that Blane had seldom seen anyone—and that, when dead, he had looked so different. She had provided the clues which Mannering hadn't picked up.

He drove towards St. John's Wood, parked the car outside Mrs. Webber's house, went up the drive, and saw the front door opening as he neared it. Mrs. Webber welcomed him without any fuss.

" Good job you weren't five minutes later," she said. " The chips would have spoiled. Mrs. Mannering and Josh are in the parlour. We're using the big round table, as there's that Mr. Chittering as well. Everything okay now ? "

Mannering saw Lorna through the window, Larraby and Chittering with glasses in their hands.

" Everything's wonderful," he said.